Out of Reach

By

Missy Johnson

Dedication

To everyone who has loved and lost, and found
the strength to move on.

Other books by Missy

Always You

Tease

Promiscuous (Tease #2)

Seduce (Beautiful Rose #0.5)

Beautiful Rose

Provoke

Inseparable

So Many Reasons Why

Desire

Anthologies

Forbidden Fruit

Risqué

Breakaway

Connect with Missy

Website: www.missycjohnson.com

Twitter: @MissycJohnson

www.facebook.com/MissycJohnson

Prologue

Andy

Death. It is the only certainty in life.

It's such a small word that holds such a powerful message. We avoid talking about it and we fear it, because we're taught to do so, because nobody really knows what happens when you die. It's that uncertainty that is so terrifying.

It's amazing how being told you're going to die puts things into perspective.

How being told your body is going to slowly give up on you makes you reevaluate everything you thought you knew. Things you take for granted suddenly seem so fragile. The worst part isn't the thought of dying itself, it's everything you're going to be leaving behind.

My name's Andy Grayson. I'm twenty-six, and I'm dying. God, saying that still freaks me out. I don't know how long I have left. A month—maybe two, if I'm lucky. For a long time, I was angry: I've been fighting this fucking disease since I was seventeen and it's finally going to win. I have nothing else to fight with because it has taken everything.

Then I realized that this is no longer about me. I can't save myself, but I can make sure the people I love are taken care of. This became less about what I was losing, and more about what I could gain.

That's when I decided I was going to do this on my terms.

Em is my girlfriend and I love her with everything I have in me. She isn't just my girl, though; she's my one of my best friends, my lover, my confidante, my partner in crime, and there isn't anything I wouldn't do for her.

And then there's Seth: we've been best friends for so long he's like a brother to me, and I know he feels the same. As kids we got into more trouble than I care to mention, and before I die I intend on getting him into some more—for old times' sake and all that shit.

Without them by my side, I wouldn't have fought for this long. They sacrificed so much for me and now it's time for me to return the favor.

I can't leave them without knowing the two people closest to my heart will be okay. I need that assurance before I settle back and let this fucking disease take me— finish me off for all eternity…

Chapter One

Seth

"You want me to what?"

I watched as Andy hoisted himself from the edge of the bed and into his chair. He winced in pain, which in turn made me cringe. I couldn't even imagine how much he would be hurting right now. He sighed, closing his eyes as he struggled to catch his breath, his white shirt and sweat pants hanging off his thin frame.

"You heard me. I'll be fucked if I'm going to spend my last days cooped up in this place, or worse: a hospital." He said *hospital* like it was a dirty word. I guess when you'd spent a good part of the last year there, it was.

"Dude, there is no way your mom is going to let—"

"Which is why you're going to pick me up tonight after they are asleep," he cut in, his eyes wide with excitement. *The hell I am.* He smiled one of his trademark smiles that you couldn't help but return.

He can smile all he wants; this is a stupid idea.

Andy's parents loved me like a son. They'd forgive me for almost anything, but this? They would *kill* me for this.

Andy's face softened as he looked at me. "Please, man. I need this," he urged.

I sighed. How could I say no to that? He was the one dying, not me. What right did I have, telling him how he should spend his last few weeks?

"Fine," I muttered, giving in. "Where do you want to go?" I sat down on the edge of his bed and glanced around the room. The smell of disinfectant was strong, and both the bedside and dressing tables were piled high with medications. I'd spent so much of my childhood inside this room, from plotting how to take over the world to discussing girls, sex, and video games. Now all those memories felt like a lifetime ago.

We'd been best friends since we were thrown together for a school assignment when we were eight. We were complete opposites. Andy was loud and funny. He loved being the center of attention, whereas I preferred to hide in the background.

He was like a brother to me. I'd do anything for him— even break him out of home, if that's what it took to make his last few weeks comfortable.

Fucking cancer. He'd been fighting it since it first reared its ugly head when we were seventeen. What seventeen-year-old worries about shit like a tiny, barely visible mole on the inside of his big toe? Apparently Andy should have, because by the time they discovered the melanoma it had already spread to his pancreas.

Treatment had gone well initially: the intense radiation and chemo had shrunk the tumor, and a biopsy had caught most of the infected tissue around the mole. He had gone into remission the week before my twenty-first birthday. Then, nearly a year ago, a routine scan found the cancer was back. More tumors developed on his lungs and in his liver, which meant more chemo, more radiation, and now it had come to this. There was nothing else they could do but manage the pain. At best, they thought he had maybe a month left. The cancer was everywhere now: in his brain, his lungs, his liver, on his spine . . . everything was slowly beginning to shut down. He was dying.

"Everything is booked and paid for. All you guys have to do is get me out of here." He grinned and cocked his head sideways, running his fingers through his short-cropped hair. "You can handle that, right? I mean, I know you have trouble with doing anything fun," he joked. I flipped him my middle finger as he laughed. "Dude, I'm gonna miss your ugly face."

"You'll be dead," I retorted, a heavy weight growing in my chest. "You're not going to miss shit."

We joked about it, but I couldn't imagine life without Andy. The thought of not being able to pick up the phone and call him, or come over and watch the game with him didn't feel real. Who was I going to make fun of for doing stupid and pointless things, if not Andy? Who was I going to do stupid and pointless things *with*?

"So Em is coming too?" I asked, clearing my throat, trying to keep my tone neutral. Just saying her name had my heart racing, but that was nothing new. Everything about that girl made me crazy. Whether she was there in front of me, or in my dreams, her beauty, her strength, and her determination never failed to amaze me. My grandmother used to tell me that I'd know when I was in love, because every action and thought would be done with that person in mind. That summed up how I felt about Em.

Andy snorted. "Of course she's coming. You think my parents will be unforgiving? Em would fucking *murder* you if we left without her." He chuckled, his dry, cracked lips forming a smile.

That was an understatement. She might have been Andy's girlfriend, but the three of us did pretty much everything together, and had since we were kids. I ran my hand through my thick hair, trying to process everything. I'd need to take leave from work. If they didn't approve it, I would just quit. Nothing was more important than Andy right now.

For the past nine months I'd been working at a law firm that specialized in corporate law for. Most people would find what I did boring, but I loved it. By most people, I meant Andy. He'd also studied law, but he had much higher aspirations than me. His eyes had been on the courtroom, the biggest cases—the ones that captured the headlines. Andy loved the spotlight, and I didn't doubt he would've gotten there, too, if it hadn't been for his illness.

"Okay, so when are we doing this?"

Andy's mouth spread into a grin. He slumped forward in his chair, his eyes narrowing in on mine. "How's tomorrow work for you?"

"Tomorrow?" I repeated, laughing. I shouldn't have been surprised: springing something like this on me last-minute was a very Andy thing to do.

"Yeah, sorry about the short notice, but it's not like I'm spoiled for time." He smirked, his eyes sparkling at me.

I sighed and shook my head. Always making a joke, even when it came to his own life and death. *Has he even considered the fact that he was dying in a serious light?* I immediately felt bad. Could I be any more condescending?

"Whatever you want, man. I figure you have a plan for your parents?"

Andy laughed. "Dad will be away at work. You'll be picking Em and I up at four. Mom takes some pretty heavy sleeping pills at night, so she won't hear a thing."

"And if she does?" I smirked, raising my eyebrows.

"She won't," he replied, confident.

"She's going to kill you. You know that, right?"

"I'll be dead. It's you she's going to kill." He chuckled.

Yeah, he could joke about it, but that's exactly what she was going to do.

***

I walked into my bedroom and pulled out my suitcase from the top shelf of my closet. With no idea where we were going or for how long, I packed enough to last me a couple of weeks.

Zipping it shut, I threw it on the floor and walked out into the kitchen. *Fuck.* I ran my hands through my hair, my fingers massaging the back of my neck. What else did I need to do? And what the hell was I going to tell work?

The easiest thing to do was just to call in sick and hope it didn't ruin my chances for the promotion I was up for next month. Hell, even if it did . . . who cared? This was probably my last chance to spend time with my best friend. They could fire me for all I cared. I could get another job; I'd never find another Andy.

I leaned over the kitchen counter, cradling my head in my hands. Life wasn't fair. He was only twenty-six, and he was dying. There were so many healthy assholes in the world, and he was going to be dead in a month.

How the hell was Andy so relaxed about everything? I

was an absolute wreck, and Emily . . .

Sighing, I rubbed my forehead. This was going to be painful.

Emily. I avoided situations that had me in close proximity to her alone for long periods of time, because the more time I spent with her, the harder it became to ignore my feelings.

I hated the situation I was in. I felt trapped, backed into a corner I'd never be able to escape from. Emily and I could never work. Even after he was gone, I would be too much of a reminder of what she'd lost. I laughed bitterly. Who even thinks like that? What kind of asshole was I? *The kind who has been in love with his best friend's girl for over fourteen years.*

My phone vibrated. I picked it up, expecting Andy. It wasn't.

"Seth?"

My throat closed over as her sweet voice drifted through the speaker. The sound of her voice, her name, her loyalty to Andy . . . everything about Em, I loved. Every day was a struggle to pretend things were normal, when they weren't.

"Are you there?"

"Yeah, sorry. Em, how are you?" I said, cringing at how foolish I sounded. I'd had no problem masking my feelings for the last fourteen years; why was it so hard all of a sudden?

"Good. I just wanted to check things were all good for tomorrow," she said. She sounded tired. Stressed. "I'm assuming he spoke to you?"

"Yeah." I hesitated, not sure whether to say what was on my mind. "Do you think it's a good idea? I mean, he's really sick. And you know Deb is gonna freak out," I added, referring to his mom. Deb was like a second mother to me, and the thought of robbing her of her last days with her son made me feel sick.

"It's what he wants," Em said. Her voice was so soft I barely heard her.

And just like that, I was back to feeling like the world's biggest asshole. Andy deserved to decide for himself how he wanted to spend his last few weeks. If that meant working extra hard on pushing my feelings aside, then I'd do it. I'd do anything for him. And I knew Emily would, too.

"You're right," I muttered. "Okay, let's do this. I'll be at his mom's place at four."

"See you then."

"Yeah," I said, closing my eyes and imagining her face. "See you then."

***

At four on the dot, I pulled up outside Seth's mom's house. I'd barely slept, my mind running on overdrive trying to process all that was happening.

Exiting the car, I shivered and zipped up my thick black jacket. The street was quiet, with only the faint sound of traffic in the distance. In the darkness I could just make out Em waiting outside for me. I walked over to her. I didn't notice the way her long hair rustled in the breeze. Or how pink her cheeks were from the cold. And I definitely didn't notice how sexy she looked in her tight-fitting jeans and red wool jacket.

My throat tightened as she wrapped her arms around my neck, kissing me softly on the cheek. I inhaled slowly, taking in as much of her scent as I could. God, it felt so good having her in my arms.

"Ready?" I asked, pulling away from her.

She smiled and nodded. "Yep. We're all packed and ready to go." Her upbeat tone didn't match the sadness in her eyes. What was she thinking? If she was like me, she probably couldn't get it out of her head that this might be his last trip. Squeezing her hand, I wished I could take the pain away from her. But I couldn't. There were no words, no actions that could make any of this okay.

I followed her in through the side door and down the hall to Andy's room. He sat in his chair, waiting. His face lit up when he saw me, like he'd been waiting all night. He looked good—better than he had yesterday. Or maybe that was just the bad lighting in his room.

"Good, let's get moving," he said, rubbing his hands together. "So little time, so much planned."

I laughed. I had no idea what he meant by that, and Andy being Andy, I probably didn't *want* to know. I stepped behind him and pushed the chair forward. It jumped along the carpet, catching on a loose thread, nearly knocking Andy out of the seat.

"Dude," he hissed. He reached down and released the brake on his chair. "Seriously. Have you never pushed one of these before?"

"Geez, excuse me for not knowing the ins and outs of your fucking chair," I muttered as I pushed him down the hall. I was stressed enough as it was.

14

With every creak of the floorboards below us, my heart stopped as I waited for Deb to jump out and catch us. But it never happened. Soon we were standing by the car, Emily to my left, as we loaded Andy into the back seat of my Chrysler along with enough pillows and blankets to service a small motel. His hands gripped the gray vinyl material of the back seat as he struggled to position himself.

"Crap," he cursed, fumbling in the pockets of his dark blue wool robe. He pulled out a crumpled piece of paper and thrust it into my hands. I glanced down, shocked at how cold his fingers were. They were like ice. "Can you leave this on the kitchen counter for me? I don't want Mom to worry." He looked away, like he was embarrassed for caring.

"Sure. I'll be back in a second."

Turning, I walked back up the path, the note in my hand as I snuck back inside the side door. Shuffling for my keys, I pulled them out and turned on the key-ring flashlight I'd bought and never used until now. Finally it was coming in handy. I was snooping, but I needed to know how much he was telling her. As soon as she realized we were gone she would be calling and texting all three of us in a panic, and I had no idea how I was going to avoid speaking to her.

I placed the note on the counter, smoothing out the creases.

Mom,

Please don't be angry with me. You know how much I love you and Dad, I just needed to do this. And please don't be angry at Seth and Emily. You know I always get my way.

I love you.

Andy xx

I sighed and left the note. I still didn't agree with what he was doing, but if he was going to do this, we were going to be by his side. He knew when he asked me, I couldn't say no. I'd never been able to, even when we were kids. He'd guilt me into his stupid and random plans every fucking time. He was also stubborn enough to have just called a taxi and gone off somewhere alone, which would've meant Em and I chasing him across the country anyway. Besides, I knew that eventually Deb would forgive me.

I just wasn't sure I'd forgive myself if he died without her being able to say goodbye.

Chapter Two

Emily

"Are you warm enough?" I tugged at the blankets covering Andy. I was cold. I wasn't sure how he couldn't be. He rolled his eyes and pushed the blankets back down, annoyed at my fussing.

"I'm fine, Em. Stop stressing," he said. He reached up and traced along the side of my cheek. "You're the one who's cold. You're shivering. Maybe you need some Andy loving to warm you up," he teased, wiggling his eyebrows.

I leaned down to kiss him, forcing myself to smile at his joke. "No," I said, putting my hands up to stop him as he tried to push one of the blankets onto me. "Just do what you're told for once," I muttered, kissing him on the nose.

"Right, because you always do what I tell you." He laughed, but let me tuck the blankets back around him.

"That's different," I replied smugly, folding his hand into mine. "You're skin and bones. It's not like you could stop me."

"Harsh," he said, a faint smile on his lips. His gaze fell downward. "Em? Thanks for this. What you and Seth are doing for me means a lot."

"I know it does." My voice dropped. The tightness in my chest became more apparent. It was always there: a gnawing feeling, like I was just waiting for something bad to happen. And I guess I was.

I remember the day of his diagnosis like it was yesterday. I remember sitting in that office with him and Deb as the doctor explained how the melanoma they'd found on his little toe had spread to his pancreas. The prognosis wasn't good, but it could have been worse. There was hope.

Until there wasn't.

Terminal. Hearing that word, I still clung to hope that a miracle would happen, and that somehow the cancer would shrink. I'd lost my parents; surely life couldn't be this cruel, could it? I felt awful even thinking about myself. I couldn't imagine how he must have felt. He'd fought so hard for so long, and to be told there was nothing more they could do . . . how do you process that?

"Em," Andy said. "Good thoughts, remember?"

I smiled, blinking back tears as I reached inside my jacket pocket and touched the small leather binder. *Good thoughts*. When it was obvious I wasn't coping, I'd begun writing down a list of memories, forcing myself to only focus on the good. It had been Andy's idea, a way for me to remember the time we'd had together—the time we had left. It was my way of staying strong for him, because the last thing he needed was for me to be a broken mess. If I let myself slow down for even a second, then that's exactly what I'd be.

"Good thoughts," I mumbled, squeezing his hand.

"This will be great, I promise." He lifted his hand and let his fingers run through my hair. "You're so beautiful, Em. Do you have any idea how much I love you?"

"I have a fair idea," I said, my heart skipping. I leaned down and placed my mouth on his. He kissed me back, his lips softly moving in sync with mine as my fingers raked through his short dark hair. I pulled away and smiled before moving back in for another kiss.

"You can't get enough of me," he said tenderly. "See? I'm irresistible."

"You are," I agreed, giggling. I stood back up, resting my back against the open door of the car, my hand still draped in his.

But behind my laughter was pure agony, because every kiss left me wondering if there would be another. Every moment we spent together could well be our last, and that meant I had to make every moment count.

Chapter Three

Seth

"All done."

"Did you read it?" asked Andy, raising an eyebrow.

"Of course I did," I retorted. I shook my head and opened the driver's side door. "Your mom is going to me calling non-fucking-stop once she realizes you're gone."

"Yeah. She's going to be pissed," he agreed.

That was the understatement of the century.

I slid inside and shut the door, starting up the car as Em slipped in beside me. Her blue eyes met mine and she smiled, running her fingers through her long, dark hair. God, how I longed to be the one doing that. Touching her.

Kissing those plump, red lips. I loved the way she smiled. And the way her bottom lip caught under her tooth when she was nervous or deep in thought.

"Dude," Andy's voice sliced through my thoughts. "Are you trying to get me caught?"

"Sorry," I muttered, stepping on the accelerator. My eyes fell on Em's long, slender fingers as she reached for the stereo knob. Her nails were painted a light pink. I smiled as *Jesse's Girl* blared through the speakers.

How appropriate. If I had an anthem, this song would be it.

Glancing in the rearview mirror, I saw Andy was fast asleep. We'd barely made it out of his street, and he was out like a light. I glanced at his chest, watching for a sign that he was still breathing. *Still alive.* I sighed with relief when a burst of air exited his lungs.

"I do that, too."

I glanced sideways at Em, who was watching me. The sadness in her eyes made me hurt. My chest burned like I'd swallowed a cup full of battery acid.

"Every night, I watch him sleep. He looks so peaceful that I have to check . . . to make sure . . ." She didn't finish.

She didn't have to. We both knew what she meant.

"I think it's a natural instinct, to want to protect him," I mumbled, the words flowing thickly past my lips.

"I imagine that's what it's like to have a baby. Those first few weeks where every moment they sleep, you worry." She laughed lightly. "I'd make the worst mother. I'd be in there shaking her awake, just to make sure she was still with me. Or him."

"You'd make the best mother," I replied, my voice soft.

She smiled at me again, her green eyes lighting up.

"It's true." I shrugged. "You're one of the most caring people I know."

"Thanks. Though I feel like I'll never . . . I don't know. You don't need to hear this." She turned away from me, staring out the window, trying to hide the tears that were rolling down her cheeks.

I wanted to comfort her. I so badly wanted to just take her in my arms and tell her everything was going to be all right, but I was frozen. I was unable to move, my hands clutching the steering wheel, my mind unable to focus on anything other than Andy, sprawled out on my back seat.

I was an asshole. The worst kind of friend.

Because my want to help her, that desire to be there for her was so strong . . . I could paint it however I liked: deep down I knew that it had less to do with being a good friend and everything to do with being that person that she needed.

Lifting my hand off the wheel, I reached over and touched her arm. She jumped, but let my fingers trail down to hers. I held her hand and tried to force myself not to think about the electricity pulsating through my body at the feel of her touch. It was hopeless. It was like standing in a rainstorm and pretending you weren't getting wet. It was impossible for my body not to react to her.

"It'll be okay, Em. I'll be here for you—for both of you."

"I don't know how you're so calm," she replied. Gathering her hair over one shoulder, she sighed. "I'm a mess. Every time I kiss him I wonder if it will be our last. I can't sleep, because what if he goes in the middle of the night, and I'm not there for him?"

"You're going to run yourself into the ground." Into the ground? I cringed. *Great choice of words.*

"At least then I won't be alone," she whispered. That

was it. She never stopped, because when she did the reality became all too real.

"You'll never be alone. You'll always have me. And Deb, and Karl."

She nodded, a smile plastered on her lips, but the sadness in her eyes remained. I knew it wasn't the same, but she had no idea how loved she actually was. She thought losing Andy would make her alone, but that was so far from the truth. And she would never know that.

Because if there was one thing worse than being in love with your dying best friend's girl, it was telling her that after he was gone.

Chapter Four

Emily

We'd been driving for hours. Andy still hadn't given us an exact address, but I suspected we were headed for the beach. I wasn't sure why, but it just seemed like a very *Andy* place to go to die.

When I used to visit him on the weekends back in college, we'd get up early and lay on the beach, tangled in each other's arms, watching the sunrise. Those moments had been perfect. He'd beaten cancer once, so in my eyes he was invincible.

I'd give anything to be able to erase those memories and experience them all again for the first time. To experience again how romantic he could be, or how sweet his kisses could taste. Or how it could feel like the whole world stopped when my head rested against his chest and I listened to the beat of his heart.

Or how broken I would be without him.

But I couldn't, and as hard as it was, I had to try and make these last few weeks special for him. It was selfish for me to think of myself when he was the one dying.

**

I quickly reached across and punched Seth square in the shoulder. *Hard.* He laughed as I pointed to the red Jeep that was flying past us in the other direction. Andy was still sleeping, and Seth and I had resorted to childish car games to pass the time.

His fist came out of nowhere and connected with my arm. I instinctively grabbed at it, my eyes narrowing in on him. He nodded ahead to the silver Jeep in front of us. I laughed. Shit. *How did I miss that one?*

"Okay, we need a new game or you're going to end up covered in bruises," he said, his lips turning up into a cocky grin.

I narrowed my eyes at him, trying to hide my amusement. "Me? You're getting just as many punches as I

27

am," I retorted.

He laughed. "True, but you hit like a girl."

My mouth fell open. Reaching over, I punched him as hard as I could in the arm. He yelped, sending a little thrill of satisfaction rushing through me. I giggled as he shook his head.

Turning to check on Andy, I felt a wave of guilt hit me.

Laughing had become so foreign to me. Pretending to be happy: now that was something I'd mastered. But actual happiness? That feeling that races through you when you think about how perfect a moment is? That was rare. It was like those moments stopped existing the second I found out Andy was dying.

I felt bad about laughing. I shouldn't have been feeling happy. Happiness and laughter were feelings reserved for moments of hope and joy. Nothing about this situation exuded that.

"What's wrong?"

I glanced at Seth, surprised he'd noticed. But then again, he always noticed. He knew me so well.

"From laughing and smiling to on the verge of tears in ten seconds flat. Talk to me, Em."

I shrugged, not trusting myself with words. If I opened my mouth right then, all that would spill out would be a jumbled, sobbing mess. I couldn't imagine my life after Andy. He had been sick for nine years, terminal for six months. I should have felt prepared, but how can you ever be ready for that?

Just when I thought I had myself under control, I'd remember, or do something, that would remind me of Andy and the fact that I was losing him. My heart was a mess, and my head was confused. I didn't know what I should be feeling. Or how I should be acting. I was mourning him and he wasn't even gone yet.

"I'm here. Whenever you need to talk, I'm here for you. Always." Seth reached over and squeezed my hand. I managed a smile, comforted by his words.

Seth.

The boy who had been as big a part of my life as Andy had been since we were twelve. The three of us, against the world.

I snuck a look his way. His hands gripped the wheel, his eyes firmly on the road. His dark mop of hair was wild and unruly, but it suited him. He was attractive, kind, and funny, yet he'd never had a serious relationship. I didn't question it, because what business was it of mine? Of course I'd spoken to Andy about it, who had laughed and shrugged it off as him just not having found the right girl. How do you find the right girl when you're not even looking?

Relaxing into my seat, I tried to fight the sleepiness that was overcoming me. I glanced behind me at Andy, who was propped up on his pillows, legs sprawled across the back seat. I swallowed the golf-ball-sized lump in my throat. He looked so peaceful when he slept. He never complained about the pain, even though I could see it in his eyes every time he moved. He was so desperate to protect me from what was happening to his body, but how could he? Nothing was going to change the path he was on.

Shifting back around in my seat, my eyes locked briefly with Seth's. I forced a small smile, knowing it wouldn't fool him. He knew me better than almost anyone. *Almost.* Soon that "almost" wouldn't apply anymore. Soon he would be all I had.

"There's a truck stop just up here. We should stop for a drink. I could use a caffeine hit."

I nodded, not bothering to feign interest. I mean, what

was the point? That was my attitude a lot these days. Though I tried not to show it, I was losing faith in life and humanity. Life was just a game and the end result was death. There was no way around that. No restarting things because you were playing it badly. You had one shot, and that was it. I wasn't sure I wanted to play anymore.

I'd lost both my parents when I was fourteen to a car accident. The last words I spoke to my mother were, "I wish I'd been born to someone else." And all because she'd refused me a pair of three-hundred-dollar jeans.

For a long time, I'd hated myself. I hated the person I was, and I'd blamed myself for not being a better daughter. When I was little, every night, I'd kiss my parents goodnight and tell them I loved them. I would end every phone call with *I love you*. As soon as we moved to Chicago, all that had changed. And when I started high school, I wanted to be a different person. I was sick of the goody-two-shoes persona I had going on. I wanted to rebel.

I was a normal teenager, acting like a normal teenager— only I hadn't expected not being allowed the chance to rectify my behavior. Every teenager acts up. Then you look back on it and laugh. You don't expect to lose everything.

The worst thing was, in the trunk of the car was a bag

from Diesel, with my three-hundred-dollar pair of jeans.

I still have them now, still unworn, wrapped in tissue paper and charred from the wreckage. Still sitting in a box under my bed as a constant reminder to myself to never let those you love go a day without hearing those words.

"Em?"

I looked up. Seth was staring at me. Glancing around, I realized we'd pulled into a truck stop. I looked out the window, embarrassed that he'd caught me lost in my own thoughts. The parking lot was nearly deserted, apart from an older couple getting into a beat-up old Dodge two spots away from us. I watched the man as he leaned in and kissed her on the cheek. She smiled up at him with love in her eyes. My heart sank. That would never be us. Andy I weren't going to grow old together. There were so many things we'd never get to do.

"Sorry," I muttered, unbuckling my seatbelt. Getting out of the car, I opened the passenger door. Andy roused as I gently shook his shoulder. "Hey, baby. Do you need anything?" I asked, my voice soft. He winced in pain and my heart broke for him. I wanted to burst into tears because I couldn't make everything right.

He was a shadow of the man I'd fallen in love with all

those years ago. His skin was so pale; it almost looked translucent in the soft glow of the morning light. His beautiful eyes, once so dark and full of life, were now dull, and hiding so much pain. His dark hair, short and thin, had grown back since the chemo had stopped, but it was nothing like the lustrous, curly locks he'd once had.

He hesitated, his eyes dropping. "I need help . . ." He broke off, embarrassed. I nodded and assisted him out of the car. He didn't need to say it. Nowadays, it was a regular occurrence.

"Do you need your chair?" I asked.

Seth appeared by my side. "Anything I can do to help?"

"He needs to go to the bathroom," I replied quickly.

Andy glanced down, his face coloring.

"Oh, well I can help him—"

"No," I cut in, a little too loudly. Andy cringed as I struggled to come up with an excuse that wouldn't embarrass him. Only I couldn't think of one. "It's just . . . I . . ."

"I've already *gone* to the bathroom, man. Trust me. You don't want any part of this," Andy mumbled, flicking at a piece of lint on his track pants.

"Oh," Seth replied, leading us into an awkward silence.

"Can you get the wheelchair out?" I asked him.

He nodded and jumped into action, racing around the back of the car and popping open the trunk.

"Thanks." I smiled as he wheeled it around.

I helped Andy over into the chair and grabbed his bag.

"Can you get me a coffee and something to eat?" I asked Seth as he walked alongside me into the truck stop.

"Sure, what to eat?"

"A bagel or something easy."

He nodded. "Anything for you, man? I can get them to put a shake and burger in the blender for you," he added with a grin. Andy burst out laughing. Just like that, the weirdness of the situation vanished.

"Only if you drink it too," he shot back.

Seth screwed up his nose. "I think I'll pass on that."

A sigh escaped me as I pushed Andy over to the restrooms. I hated things being awkward between the three of us. One of the things I loved most about Seth was that he didn't change around Andy. He was still the same wisecracking smartass. It was as though Andy's dying wasn't an issue. He didn't hesitate to crack a cancer joke, or talk about guy stuff. He kept things real, and I knew how much Andy appreciated that.

"What do you need?" I asked, reversing the chair against the bench in the small shower room. The stench of mold and urine hung in the air, masked by the overpowering smell of disinfectant.

It might seem like a romance killer, but I'd been changing his catheter bags and wiping his ass for the past few months. It was almost second nature for me now. I knew that was a big reason behind his decision to move back home with his parents: he didn't want to burden me with all of that. I also think it upset him, thinking about how much our relationship had changed. I had gone from his girlfriend to his caregiver. I hated being that person. I hated seeing him so broken. But as hard as it was for me to handle, it paled in comparison to what he was going through, and for that reason alone I forced myself to work through it.

"If you pass me the towel in the bag, I'll be okay."

"No, let me help—"

"Em, I'll be fine. Please." His expression softened as

soon as he saw the hurt in my eyes. "I'm sorry. I can't have you doing this for me. I can't handle having my girlfriend wiping my ass every time I shit my pants, okay?"

I backed off. He was frustrated and I got it, but he needed help. Did he think I liked seeing him like this?

"You need help, Andy. How are you going to get through this trip if you won't let me help you?" I asked, crossing my arms over my chest.

"I've hired a nurse," he said, not meeting my eyes.

He'd *what?* How could he do something like that without talking with me about it first? My heart ached. Why was he pushing me away?

"Em," he said, reaching for my hand. "I want this trip to be something you remember. This isn't about me. I'm dying. I'm okay with that. This is about me not wanting your final memories of me to be filled with the bad. Focus on the good, remember?"

I smiled through my tears. *Focus on the good.* If only it were that easy.

Chapter Five

Seth

"Turn right up here, and then go straight to the end of the road. There should be a track to your left."

I followed Andy's directions, marveling at some of the huge houses we passed along the way. With lush, green sprawling lawns and perfectly-manicured gardens, everything was stunning. I felt out of place in my old, piece-of-shit car.

"What the hell, Andy? Millicent?" Em sighed, rolling her eyes.

Millicent was one of the most expensive holiday destinations in the state. This was where people with money came to relax, where the teenaged spawn of people with money came to party. A rental here must've cost him a shitload.

Andy shrugged, a grin on his face. "What's the point of money in the bank if I'm dying?"

I shot a look toward Em. Her eyes were dark. She looked annoyed, and I felt her pain. I was angry that he would blow his life savings without any consideration for her. *He* was dying; she wasn't. She had debts, many of which had been run up because she couldn't work full time while caring for Andy when he was really sick.

"That's a great attitude to have," I muttered.

"Geez, Seth. Relax, okay? Don't go all Mr. Responsible on me. I think if I've ever been entitled to let loose a little, it's now."

"Come on, when have you *ever* held back?" I scoffed. "Your whole life has been one party after the next." As soon as the words fell out of my mouth, I regretted them.

"Yeah," he muttered, "because dying of cancer is such a party. You should try it sometime."

"I'm sorry, man. I didn't mean that—"

"Yeah you did. And it's okay. But I need to do this. And I need you guys here with me, whether you agree with what

I'm doing or not."

"Fine," I said, "but at least let me front some of the cost."

"No." He shook his head, and I knew there was no point in arguing. "This is my way of thanking you guys, okay? Trust me." He nodded straight ahead. "It's that brick place down the end."

I pulled into the gated driveway and punched in the code that Andy read out. The gate swung open, allowing me to drive through.

Holy shit. The place was amazing. The cobbled driveway swerved though the heavily-treed front yard right up to the front door, accessed via a ramp instead of steps.

"Wheelchair-friendly," Andy assured me, as if reading my mind.

"Andy, this place is beautiful," Em breathed. She was right: it was fucking stunning. And it was hard to stay mad at him knowing that this was our home for the next couple of weeks.

"Wait till you see inside. And the private beach out back."

"How much is this costing you?" Em asked, her voice

nervous.

"We've been through this." He sighed. "Forget about money and just enjoy yourselves. For me. Please?"

She made a face, but nodded.

After parking the car, we got out. I helped Andy into his chair and pushed him up the ramp while Em grabbed our bags. When we reached the front door, I took the key from Andy's jacket and slipped it into the lock. The huge, hand-crafted wooden doors swung open.

Wow. And I'd thought the outside was impressive.

The place was huge—as in my entire apartment could fit in the entry kind of huge. Big windows donned the back wall, which I was sure would showcase the breathtaking view of the beach. Pity it was so late. An oversized deck, complete with Jacuzzi and a daybed, curled around the back, lit up with strings of lights.

The kitchen was all stainless steel and black marble, which tied in nicely with the black leather sofas and huge flat-screen television in the living area. It was the kind of place you'd expect to see while flipping through a *Home Beautiful* magazine.

"This is fucking unbelievable," I said, running my

fingers along the soft leather of one of the sofas. My place at home was nice and all, but this . . . this was epic. I turned just in time to see the look on Em's face as she walked inside. Her mouth fell open, and then curved up into a grin as she took in the room.

Maybe this trip wasn't going to be as bad as I'd thought. This could be just what Em needed: to get away from everything. Have a little fun.

"Holy crap, I'm in love." She sighed. She dropped our bags beside the TV and walked over toward the deck. She placed her hands on the window and stared out, her warm breath clouding over the glass. "I could stay here forever," she said.

My chest tightened. This would be Andy's forever.

"I hate to be a party pooper, but I need a nap. Can't get drunk if I can't stay awake, right?"

"Drunk?" I repeated, nearly choking on the word.

Andy nodded, a grin spreading across his lips. "What's a beach party without alcohol? You just wait, Seth. You think this is going to be about me lying in bed wishing my life were different? Fuck that, man. You know me better than that."

He was right: I *did* know him better than that, which was what worried me. He acted so strong, like he was ready for what was coming, but I wondered how much of that was an act. Death scared the hell out of me. Apart from my grandparents, who'd died before I was born, I hadn't had anyone close to me die. Andy dying terrified me. How could he not be scared?

"This is about me forgetting I'm dying. Right now I'm alive, so I'm going to live. Or at least, going to live vicariously though you guys," he added cryptically, his eyes narrowing as he chuckled.

"Oh God. What are you planning?" I groaned, growing more and more nervous by the minute.

"You'll see." He grinned. "But trust me. You guys are never going to forget me. I'm going to make sure of it."

I snorted, my eyes meeting Em's. She smiled back.

As if we could ever forget him.

***

Sitting at the kitchen table, I glanced up at Em as she walked into the room. She looked tired, her eyelids heavy with dark circles around them. Her long, dark hair hung over her shoulders, reaching halfway down her back. I inhaled sharply, her beauty breathtaking. I could've stared at her all day. Every time I saw her it was like I was seeing her for the first time. I forced myself to look away, back down to the newspaper I was reading.

"How is he?" I asked, reading the same line over and over.

She shrugged, grabbing a soda from the fridge. "You know Andy. Even if he wasn't fine, he'd say he was." It was true: anything, if it meant not worrying Em or I.

"How are *you*?" I asked, the words tumbling from my mouth in a rush. Sometimes it felt like I couldn't even get my words straight around her. One look from her, one smile, and everything in my head felt jumbled. You'd think I'd be used to that feeling by now. I wasn't. I didn't think I'd ever get used to it. I wasn't sure if I wanted to.

"I'm okay," she said, shrugging. She walked around the table, pulling out the chair next to me, and sat down. Her perfume drifted past my senses: soft and delicate, just like her.

I stared down at the newspaper again, only now taking in the line I'd been reading for the last five minutes. *The Twilight Carnival comes to town.*

"Anything interesting?" Emily asked, her lips forming a perfect circle around the opening of the soda bottle.

Oh, God. I shifted in my seat, arousal building inside of me as I imagined those lips . . . elsewhere.

"Nope," I said, the tone of my voice about three levels too high. I sounded like a teenager going through puberty. "There's a carnival one town over we can check out if you want."

He face lit up. "I've never been to a carnival," she said, her lips spreading into a grin. She fingered the rim of her bottle of soda, a wistful look in her eyes.

"How is that even possible?" I smirked. "Everyone's been to the carnival at least once. It's un-American to not have."

"Excuse me," she replied, sitting straighter in her seat. "You're calling me un-American, Mr. I-Spent-Every-Friday-Night-in-College-Studying-Rather-Than-Going-to-the-Football-Game?"

"Hey, I had exams," I protested, laughing. I was probably the only college student who took college seriously—partly because I didn't trust myself to drink around Em. College had been a weird time for me. Em studying elsewhere had made me realize how much I hated being around her, yet I couldn't imagine not being around her. Love was a fucked-up thing when it was one-sided.

"Every week?" she asked, rolling her eyes. Okay, she had me there. So I didn't see the point in watching men jumping all over one another when I needed a near-perfect score to get into law school. So what?

Andy, on the other hand, had been all about the partying. He missed more classes than he attended, usually because he was too hung-over to find his way out of bed.

He and Emily had begun dating just before college. We went to Northwestern University, while she had studied literacy at Chicago University. Em would spend nearly every weekend in our apartment.

"What have you told work?" she asked suddenly.

"Nothing yet. I'll call in sick on Monday and take it from there. I have some leave saved up, so I might try and wrangle that. You?"

Emily smiled. "That's the beauty of being a columnist. I can do it anywhere." Her eyes clouded over. "They've been really understanding, actually. My boss lost her husband to cancer a few years ago. She's been really supportive."

"Good," I smiled, "because if you needed me to go down and hit some heads, I'd do it."

She laughed. "God, Seth, you're such a dork."

"But seriously, I'm really glad they are so understanding. I guess it helps that she's been through it too, huh?"

She nodded, a small smile on her lips. "It does, actually. She's been helping me with what to expect in these last few weeks. I think I feel better knowing what's coming, if that makes sense?"

It did. And I imagined it would be much more comforting coming from someone who had been through it than relying on Google, as I had been doing. The way cancer ravaged the body in those last few days . . . the idea of that being Andy terrified the hell out of me.

"I'm pretty beat. I think I might go to bed too," Em said. I yawned, barely able to keep my eyes open.

"Yeah, it's been a long day."

"I'll see you tomorrow. Thanks for this, Seth." She kissed me on the cheek, her hands trailing down my arm as she walked away. I watched her go as her touch lingered on me.

Closing my eyes, I sighed. This was going to be hard.

Chapter Six

Emily

Two hundred and forty-eight days: that was the last time we were intimate together. I lay on the bed beside him, watching his chest slowly rise and fall with each shallow breath he took. How awful was I that sex was what was on my mind right now? Thoughts like this flew through my mind on a daily basis, and each and every time I felt like complete shit. It was like I wanted to torture myself by thinking of the things we'd lost that were out of his control. And mine.

I reached out and touched his arm. His skin, clammy and so cold, hung off him. He'd lost so much weight. Even in the last few weeks the difference was noticeable, and it scared me.

Death was something that really put things into perspective, and made all our other problems seem so trivial. I hated that he was dying; I hated that he was leaving me. I hated him for not fighting this harder. And I hated myself for even thinking about how long it had been since we were last intimate—like he had any control over that.

Most of all, I hated that our relationship had shifted. I loved Andy with every fiber of my being, but preparing someone for death does something to you. It was like my mind had gone into major protection mode, determined to shield me from as much pain as possible. Maybe it had something to do with losing my parents so young? I don't know.

I loved him so, so much, but was I still *in* love with him? I couldn't even think of answering that right now.

I can't be in here.

Creeping out of the bed, I grabbed my robe and threw it over my shoulders, lacing my arms through the sleeves. It was cold—as you'd expect at nearly five in the morning in the middle of spring. I walked out to the kitchen with my notebook and made myself a coffee. This place was huge. The kitchen was bigger than my entire apartment back home, all with the latest appliances.

I took my coffee and notebook outside onto the deck. A large daybed lay in the corner, overlooking the beach. Crawling onto it, I covered myself with blankets, trying to warm myself up.

I stared down at my notebook—my bible, as Andy called it. I'd always loved writing. When Andy got sick, my need to express myself through words became even stronger. There was something about expressing your thoughts through words on a page that was impossible to explain.

This was me nearly every night. I rarely slept, and when I did, it wasn't well. Things had gotten worse when Andy's mother insisted he move in with them. Part of me hated having to share him. How fucked up was that? It was only natural a mother would want to help her dying son, and yet I couldn't help but feel resentment toward her for that. Another part of me felt like a failure, like I couldn't look after him on my own. I guess that was because to some extent it was true.

Palliative care, as they called it, was harsh. The last few

months, his health had deteriorated so much that he needed help with everything. It was hard watching him slowly die. Because that's what I was doing. Watching. Waiting.

Only it wasn't so slow anymore.

***

The bright morning sunlight filled my eyes as I blinked them open. I must've fallen asleep. My notebook lay open, clutched in my right hand. An extra blanket had been placed over me. *Seth.* My spine tingled. I loved how much he cared for me. Without him, I would have fallen to pieces long ago.

"Morning, sleepyhead."

I sat up, eagerly accepting the cup of coffee Seth was holding out for me. I smiled shyly. He looked like he'd just woken up. His hair was all messed in a way that made me want to wet my hands and run them through it to style it into place. His blue eyes sparkled as he sat down next to me.

"Got to hand it to the old boy. He sure knows how to go all out." He gazed away from me, taking in our panoramic view of the sandy, white beach.

I nodded, watching the waves gently crash into the sand.

"It's a private beach?" I asked, realizing it was deserted. It was too beautiful for nobody to be enjoying it, even in this brisk, cool air.

"Yep. It's all ours."

I lay back, resting my head on the pillows, cradling my steaming mug in my hands. I hated mornings. I'd hated them ever since my parents died, and doubly so when Andy got sick. Every morning brought us one step closer to death.

"How're you holding up?" Seth asked quietly.

I shrugged. There was no point lying; Seth knew me too well. I snuggled in closer to him, stealing some of his warmth. He wrapped his arm around me and kissed my forehead.

"Okay," I finally replied weakly.

"Bullshit," he said, not buying it.

I rolled my eyes. What did he want me to say? Of course I wasn't okay.

"Talk to me, Em."

"What's the point?" I mumbled. His fingers closed around mine. God, he was so warm. How was he so warm?

My fingers felt like ice blocks against the heat of the cup I was holding. "Talking isn't going to change things."

"No, but it might help put things into perspective."

I laughed. "Perspective? How's this for perspective? I blame him for leaving me. I'm too scared to move on, Seth, because I'm terrified of forgetting him when he's gone."

"Nobody said you have to move on right away," he murmured, his lips brushing over my cheek. "You feel right now that you're never going to get through this, and I get it. But you will. You're an incredibly strong, amazing woman. The strongest woman I know."

A rush of excitement surged through me, hearing him say those words.

"Thanks," I mumbled, my face heating up at his words.

"Are you blushing, Em?" He nudged me and laughed. "Now that's adorable."

"Shut up," I grumbled, nudging him back so hard my coffee spilled all over the white spread. I'd only ever been with Andy. Hearing Seth say those things, even just as a friend, wakened some unexpected feelings inside of me.

The funny thing was, it had been Seth I'd been crushing on back in the beginning. I'd hang around with them, praying that he would notice me . . . but he never did. He never showed any interest, so when Andy had asked me out I'd said yes. The three of us had been inseparable, even when Andy and I had become a couple. Seth was so much a part of our relationship, it would've been weird not having him around.

Where Andy had my heart, Seth was so fiercely protective of me that I'd always felt lucky to have the both of them in my life. They were so alike, yet so different— but the one thing that remained constant was their loyalty to each other, and to me.

Chapter Seven

Emily

My eyes narrowed in on Andy as I walked into the
kitchen and sat down. He had asked both Seth and I to join
him for breakfast. It all felt so formal, especially
considering Andy's breakfast consisted of a protein shake
being fed via a PEG tube. He could eat food, but not much.
Not enough to give him the nutrition his body needed.

"What's all this about?" I asked suspiciously.

"What?" he said innocently. "I can't request a meal with
my two best friends? There are a few things I want to do,
only I'm obviously in no condition to do much, so you two
are going to do them for me."

"What?" Andy had a bucket list? He wanted us to live it

out? I shook my head. "What the hell are you talking about? What things?" This was the first I'd heard of any of it.

"You'll find out what they are as you do them. You gotta give me some fun, right?"

I narrowed my eyes at him, not trusting the sneaking little smirk on his face. What was he up to? "I'm not jumping out of any planes or doing any nudie runs," I warned.

"What? You'd deny your dying boyfriend of his final wishes?" Andy frowned. "What if I wanted you to jump out of a plane naked?"

"Then you'd be coming with me."

"Okay, fine. I'll save the skydiving and streaking for Seth. You'll do it, right, man?"

Seth shrugged. "Sure, why not?" He winked at me and I blushed, the thought of him running naked along the beach not escaping my mind. Andy narrowed his eyes at me, a thoughtful expression on his face. I cringed, embarrassed at having being caught thinking like *that* about Seth in front of Andy. Not that he would have had any idea what I was thinking, but still.

"Good man. Okay, first stop is Willows Point. We need to be there at noon."

"Why?" I already knew he wasn't likely to answer.

"Be patient, Emsky," he said patting my hand. "Oh, and wear your swimming suit." I rolled my eyes at the use of my nickname. I freaking hated it when he called me that, and he knew it.

Chapter Eight

Seth

Willows Point—home to some of the biggest cliff fronts in the northern hemisphere. I had a strange feeling in my stomach that I wasn't going to like why we were here.

"There we are," Andy announced, pointing to a van in the far corner of the lot.

I squinted to make out the sign writing: *Maximum Jump*. Oh, fuck no.

"Cliff jumping?" I gasped. "You've got to be freaking kidding me, dude."

Andy laughed. "You said you wanted to help. It's on my list." He shrugged, as if the whole thing was out of his hands. Emily stood behind Andy, giggling. "I don't know why you're giggling away, Emsky. You're doing it, too."

"The hell I am," she exclaimed, her eyes widening. I laughed at her reaction. She made a face and flipped me her middle finger.

"If you don't then I will," he threatened.

God, he's serious, too.

"Stop being such an ass, Andy." She threw him an annoyed look.

"Guys," he chastised, shaking his head. "These are things I wished I could've done. The whole idea is to live life, right? How much living have you two been doing the last few months?"

Em shifted on her seat next to me as my gaze fell downward. Fuck, he had this way of making you feel guilty for breathing.

"Fine. We'll do it." I sighed.

Em's head shot up. "We will?" she squeaked.

I took hold of her hand and gently squeezed it.

She sighed, her breathing ragged. "Okay," she said in a small voice.

"Great. This is going to be awesome. Trust me," he said as I opened my door.

"Says the guy who gets to sit in his chair and watch," I muttered.

"Ah, stop whining, Walkerson. You're being a pussy."

I laughed as I unloaded his chair. I was about to jump off a cliff, yet I was being a pussy?

Em grabbed his bag and a blanket, wrapping it around him. She looked hesitant to leave him. "Maybe I should stay with you," she said.

"No need," he replied cheerfully. He pointed to the entrance of the parking lot. I put my hand over my eyes to shield them from the sun and watched as a dark-blue Ford pulled into the spot next to us.

"Who is that?" Em asked, echoing my thoughts.

"I told you that you weren't going to spend the next few weeks stressing about me, and I meant it. That's Marta— the nurse I told you about."

Marta looked to be in her fifties. Her graying hair was pulled back into a bun. She was dressed neatly in a pair of gray slacks and a green sweater. Her mouth moved into a tight smile as she acknowledged Em and me. "I'm guessing you're Andrew?"

"What gave it away? Was it my handsome smile? Or maybe my ruggedly-built physique?" Andy grinned.

I groaned internally. Had he purposely chosen a nurse that completely reflected the opposite of his personality? Because that was something he would do.

"I must admit, when the agency told me to meet you out here I was confused." She glanced around, her eyebrows rising as she spotted the van. "And now that I'm here, I'm still confused."

"It's simple, really: I'm making these two live out my bucket list while I'm still alive enough to enjoy it."

Marta nodded slowly. "And watching them . . ." She squinted at the van. ". . . cliff-jump is going to give you joy?" she asked as she crossed her arms over her chest.

"If you knew these two, you wouldn't even have to ask. She's scared of heights," he said, pointing at Em, "and he's just a pussy."

I rolled my eyes. Marta shrugged and took control of the chair. We walked over to the van where a guy in a bright pink and orange T-shirt and ripped jeans was waiting for us. I eyed the ropes and harnesses that were piled in the back of the van.

"Hey, you must be Emily, Seth, and Andy. I'm Pete."

I shook his outstretched hand, noting his strong Australian accent. His long scruffy blonde hair was in dire need of a wash. He looked like he hadn't seen a shower in months, and his glazed over expression made me wonder if he was high.

I was supposed to trust this guy with my life?

"Nice to meet you," I said as he threw an old black wetsuit at me.

"Chuck that on. And one for you." He threw an identical one at Emily. "What about you, old girl?" he asked Marta.

She narrowed her eyes at him, crossing her arms over her chest again.

"I'll take that as a no." He chuckled. "You get changed and meet me at the van. I'll run through the jump, and then you'll be set. Cool?"

"Sure. Cool," I replied as Andy sniggered, his video camera in hand. *Yeah, laugh it up, Andy.* He was already enjoying this way too much.

Em and I got changed back over at my car. We both wore our swimsuits under our clothes, so it took literally a few seconds to strip off our clothes and pull on the wetsuits. Mine was too small and felt constricting in places I didn't want it to be. I glanced at Em, pretending I didn't notice how sexy she looked in her tight suit.

"So, you'll be harnessed to this. It's all pretty simple, really. The only thing you want to remember is when you jump, jump out—otherwise you run the risk of splattering yourself all over the rocks." The color drained from Em's face as her eyes widened. Pete laughed. "Nah, I'm kidding. It's pretty safe. The key is to pick a jump that allows for deviation."

"So there's no chance of..." Em's voice trailed off as she looked out over the cliff. If I didn't feel so sorry for her I would've laughed. She looked terrified.

"Hitting the rock? No. I've been doing this for ten years, honey. Believe it or not, I know what I'm doing."

Em blushed and took a step closer to me, her hand falling into mine. I squeezed it and gave her a wink. "I'll go first, okay? I'll be down there waiting for you."

She nodded. "Okay. Let's just get this over with."

Stepping forward, I waited as Pete hooked up my harness and ran through some last minute tips. I felt dizzy as I looked out over the drop. *Holy shit, that's a long way down.* If I said I wasn't shitting myself, I'd be lying.

"Here we go," I mumbled under my breath. One, two, three. I sprinted for the edge and jumped. For a split second, it felt like everything stopped, except for the pounding in my chest as I floated down. I hit the water with a massive splash, surfacing a few seconds later.

Holy fucking shit, that was amazing. I laughed and floated on top of the water, staring up at Em and Pete at the top of the cliff. *I can't believe I just did that.*

"Come on, Em!" I yelled as she stood back from the edge. I laughed, reliving in my mind those few seconds before the leap. And then she jumped. She screamed as she hurtled toward the water, disappearing under the surface below me.

"Oh my god." She bounced up from beneath the water, her eyes wide. "Did I really just hurl myself off a cliff?"

I laughed and began swimming toward the shore. "You did well, Em. How terrifying was it, just standing up there and looking down?"

"I know," she laughed, her cheeks flushed with color. "I just can't believe we did that."

We stumbled onto the shore and sat down on the sand. I breathed in heavily, the adrenaline still racing through my veins. I lay back and stared up at the top of the cliff. It looked even more terrifying from down here.

"That was . . . insane," I finished. Holy shit, that was up there as being one of the best experiences of my life. Rolling onto my side, I studied her as she lay there with her eyes closed. She had the biggest smile on her face I'd seen in months.

"I want to do it again." She grinned. "Do you think we can?"

I jumped to my feet and reached out for her hand, pulling her up. She stumbled into my arms. I curled them around her waist to stop her from falling. I tried to stop myself from staring at her, but it was hopeless. She looked so beautiful, with her damp, messed hair and a splash of red in her cheeks. Her hold on me didn't weaken; her eyes didn't falter. I pulled away, confused by the moment. I could've sworn there had been something there.

I had to have imagined it. There was no way . . . was there?

"Let's go find out," I said with a grin.

***

We reached the top of the cliff, courtesy of Pete's partner, Lacey, who had been waiting for us down by the water in a beat up old Honda. Andy was nowhere in sight. I saw Marta and jumped out of the car as it slowed to a stop.

"Is he okay?" I asked, worried about him.

"He's fine—he's just a little tired. Don't worry, he got the whole thing on tape," she added with a smile. "He's asked for me to take him home."

I nodded. "Of course. We'll be right behind you."

"No, he wants you to stay here. He is very insistent on you making sure the girl has fun." She lowered her voice so Em wouldn't hear. "I've only known the kid for a few hours, but he loves her. He's not concerned about himself at all. Everything is about creating memories for that one."

Memories that he *should be creating with her, not me.*

"Okay." I nodded. "Will you stay with him until we get back?"

She burst into laughter. "Honey, he's hired me to stay with him twenty-four seven."

I wondered if Em knew about that.

"What's going on? Is he okay?" Em came racing over to me as Marta walked off.

"He's fine, just tired. He wants us to keep going. Marta is going to stay for a few days, apparently."

"Oh. Okay." She took a step back, her brow creasing. I got the feeling she felt like she'd been replaced.

"Em, he wants you to have fun. He wants the last few weeks of his life to be full of memories that are going to make you smile, not cry."

"I know. I get that, it's just . . ." She shook her head. "I can't turn things off. I can't pretend everything is fine, because it's not."

"Come on. Get changed." I pushed her toward the van, my hands resting on her shoulders. She was right: nothing was going to change reality, but I was going to try my hardest to help her escape from it for at least a little while.

"Why?" she asked, unzipping her wetsuit. "I thought we were going again."

"Nope." I shrugged my own suit off and stepped out of it, reaching for my towel to wrap it around my waist. "I've got a better idea."

She groaned. "God, I've had enough of surprises for one

day," she muttered.

I grinned. I was sure she was going to like this one. My heart pounded as she lowered her wetsuit. Her black shorts clung to her like a second skin while her pink bikini top pushed up her cleavage. She reached for a towel and began to dry her hair.

Every tiny detail I noticed: the way the ends of her hair flicked trails of water down the length of her arms; the way she smiled as the sun hit her face; the way her body curved, creating the sexiest silhouette I'd ever seen.

I dragged my eyes away from her, but not before Pete met my gaze. He gave me a knowing smile. Great. I needed to pull myself together. Bundling up my clothes, I thanked Pete and told Em I'd meet her back at the car.

Pulling my T-shirt over my head, I grabbed my phone. Six missed calls. Numerous texts from Deb and my mom. I groaned. They were both going to kill me.

Flicking open a message to Mom, I texted her.

I'm doing what I need to do for Andy. Please understand. I promise to call if anything happens.

I shut my phone off. There was a pretty good chance she would try and call as soon as the message went through, and I didn't want to deal with that right now.

"Everything okay?" Em asked, sliding into the passenger's seat.

"Sure. Just going through the texts and missed calls," I said dryly.

"I brought a disposable with me." Em grinned. "I left my actual cell at home. I knew I'd cave if Deb got through to me. This way, I can't."

"Clever," I said with a smile. "Kinda sneaky, but clever."

"I can be sneaky." She smiled, buckling up her belt.

I snorted.

"What?" she said, her tone indignant. "I can be."

"Bullshit. You are way too much of a good girl," I teased.

Her cheeks colored as she leaned over and hit me. "Shut up. Ask Andy how much of a bad girl I can be," she shot back.

"I'd rather not." I made a face and she blushed an even deeper red.

"*You* have a dirty mind. I wasn't referring to anything

sexual."

"Okay, repeat what you said to me in your head. Do you blame me for thinking that was sexual?" I chuckled as she went red again. Fuck, she was adorable.

She burst out laughing. "I guess not." She glanced around. "So where are we going, anyway?"

Out of the corner of my eye, I watched her as she gathered her hair up in a loose ponytail. *Just when I thought she couldn't get any more beautiful . . .*

What would things be like after Andy was gone? I hated admitting it, but I was terrified about our friendship changing. The only thing worse than not having her as my girl was losing her altogether.

I'd never lost anyone. I had no idea how death would change our dynamics. Would seeing me remind her of Andy? My heart ached at the thought of not having her in my life.

"Seth?" Em raised her eyebrows at me.

"Huh? Sorry," I muttered. "No, I'm not telling you where we are going. But I will tell you that first we are going to get some dinner."

"And what's for dinner?" she asked suspiciously.

"Hamburgers?" I suggested. "There is a great little diner not far from the beach house."

"Hamburgers sound nice." She smiled. "Seth?" she hesitated. "Do you mind if we have dinner and then go home? I don't really feel up to anything right now."

"Sure," I said, trying to hide my disappointment. It made sense that she'd want to be with Andy while he wasn't well. And besides, the carnival would still be there tomorrow.

Andy might not.

Chapter Nine

Seth

Monday morning, the first thing I did was call work. I told them I was sick and wouldn't be in. I had a few cases coming up which I knew I'd have to finish the reports for and send them to my boss, but that could wait until later. Right now, Andy was all that mattered.

After a pretty good night's sleep, he was up and smiling. He had more color in his face, and I could see glimpses of my old friend in his eyes.

"Want to get drunk on the beach?" I asked Andy.

His eyes lit up as he grinned at me. "You'll have to carry me out there," he warned with a chuckle.

"So, not much different from college, huh?" I joked. The number of times I'd had to go haul his drunken ass home was ridiculous. "I'll get Em."

"Don't," Andy said suddenly. "I thought it would be nice just you and me."

I nodded, a little taken aback. It was rarely just him and me; it was always the three of us. I quickly scrawled down a note for her so she wouldn't worry, then went to the fridge and grabbed a six-pack of beer.

"Here," I said, giving it to him to nurse while I pushed his chair. "Do you need anything first?"

"Nope. I'm good."

I pushed the chair down to the edge of the sand and then hoisted him out and over my shoulder.

"This is fucked up, man." He laughed.

Yep, I was carrying a grown man over my shoulder. I guess it was pretty funny. Laying him down on the sand, I popped open a can and handed it to him.

"Are you sure you can drink?" I asked him doubtfully.

He shrugged. "No, but what's it going to do? Kill me?" he sniggered. *Good point.* "Marta might kill you for feeding me alcohol, though."

"Yeah, well, she can get in line," I joked.

"Has she called much? Mom?" he asked.

"Yeah. Every day. I texted my mom and told her you were fine."

"Em bought a disposable." He chuckled. "She didn't want to risk ratting me out."

"I heard," I said, shaking my head. "So . . . how are you?"

"Jesus, dude, will you stop asking me how I am?" he said, rolling his eyes. "No different from the last ten times you asked."

Shit. The thing was, I always felt like I never knew what to say. I tried to act like myself around him, like nothing was different, but it was.

I hated that I felt so useless. What was I supposed to do here? Everything was pointless. Nobody cared about the weather, or how the previous night's episode of *Game of Thrones* had been—not when there was a chance he wouldn't be around for the next. What could I possibly say right now that had any merit?

"Dude, I don't want a pity party, okay?" he shook his

head. "We've been through this before. Talk to me like I'm not dying. Joke about my bad hairdo. Make fun of how fucking sick I look. Treat me like you always do, okay? That's all I want from you."

I swallowed hard. It was such a simple request: he wanted me to be myself and treat him normally. If I couldn't manage that, then I sucked at friendship.

We sat there, both staring out at the sea, lost in thought.

Andy cleared his throat. "So, how long have you been in love with Em?"

What?

My head whipped toward him so fast I almost dislocated my neck. I couldn't have heard him right. No fucking way he'd just asked me that. Even if he knew—which was fucking impossible—why bring it up?

"What are you talking about?" I laughed, figuring it was the best response here.

Andy smiled faintly and rolled his eyes. "You don't hide it very well. Well, you try to," he corrected himself, "but I've seen the way you look at her. It's the same way I do." He didn't sound angry, just wistful. He almost sounded jealous. "Spit it out, Seth. It's not like I can beat the shit out

75

of you, is it?" he said, his voice dry. No. He could barely
lift his arms without help.

"Since the first day I saw her," I finally said, my throat
dry. My heart beat furiously as I recounted the memory.
"We were sitting in the back of Mr. Gale's class, and she
walked in late. I remember feeling like I'd been punched in
the stomach. She took my breath away. That long, dark hair
. . ." I shook my head and smiled. "I still remember what
she was wearing. A red sweater with black stripes and—"

"—a black skirt," Andy finished, his lips twitching.
"Shit, man. I had no idea. I never would've gone for her if I
knew you liked her."

I laughed. Was he kidding? He was apologizing to me?

"She loves you. And you love her. Why apologize for
that?" I shrugged as if it were no big deal. But it was.
Because their love was rare and amazing, and every
fucking day I wished it was me she was in love with.

"Because if it was you she'd fallen for, then this
would've been so much easier," he mumbled. "Because
that was eleven years ago, and you're still in love with
her." He wiped his forehead. It was cold outside, but a film
of sweat soaked his brow.

"So what?" I said. He was being ridiculous. "You think she'd change the last nine years?" I shook my head. "Not for a fucking second. You can't turn off your feelings."

"You did," he shot back.

My face flushed. No. I hadn't. That was the problem. The way I felt about Em was there, every second of the day. You can't choose who you fall in love with, but you can choose whether you act on those feelings. And I'd chosen not to.

"Because it's easy to do when the feelings aren't mutual."

He shrugged, as if he didn't completely agree. "You know, there was a moment there when I was sure she was into you. Eighth grade. She used to hang off your every freaking word. Everything was Seth this and Seth that. I was sure I had no chance with her. It's funny how things turn out."

He swished his near-full can of beer, tipping it out in a slow stream into the sand. I watched as it frothed up before soaking through the grains, disappearing into the earth. His words stuck with me. What if she had been interested in me? How different would all our lives be right now if it were me she was with today?

She was perfect in every way, and I'd spent the last fourteen years fighting my feelings for her. But she was my best friend's girl. And he was dying. Part of me hoped that meant we could someday be together.

And that made me a complete asshole.

***

"Can you get that camera out of my fucking face?" Em groaned, burying her face in the crook of her arm.

Andy laughed and continued to film her as she washed the dishes. "What? You should be flattered. I'm the one who's dying, and I'm filming you. If anything, you should be filming me."

"Like you'd ever give me control of the damn thing. It's like it's joined to your hand," she grumbled, her mouth twitching into a smile.

I chuckled. She was right. Since we'd gotten here, he'd recorded nearly every moment.

"You want it? Come get it," he taunted, his dark eyes sparkling.

"Oh yeah?" She threw off her gloves and walked over to him, bending over as he hid the camera behind his back, laughing. "You sneaky little shit." She laughed as he kissed her neck. "Give it to me."

"Come on, Em. I can barely move, and you can't get it off me? Weak." She squealed as he tickled her sides.

"Seth," Em said, lunging forward and missing the camera again, "help me. Hold him down while I get it."

I laughed. "That sounds just wrong. You want me to hold down the cripple in the chair so you can steal his camera?"

"Yeah," Andy said with a grin. "What he said."

Em rolled her eyes and stepped back, sticking her tongue out at me. I laughed. She shook her head like she didn't care, when it was so obvious she did. She didn't like to lose. The five-year-old in her came out whenever she didn't get her way, and it was hilarious to watch.

"Seriously?" She threw up her arms at Andy, who was continuing to film her.

He chuckled, setting the camera down. "Fine. Here," he said, handing it to her. "And on that note, I might go to bed." Andy yawned.

I glanced at the clock. It was barely seven.

"Big day tomorrow." He grinned, wiggling his

eyebrows.

God, why did that make me nervous? After yesterday, what else could he have planned?

Chapter Ten

Seth

The days were moving by quickly. With each day brought a new adventure, and a new way for Andy to punish Em and I. But I was okay with that, because he was happier than I'd seen him in weeks. If it took a few stupid stunts to make the last few weeks of his life a little more bearable then hell, I'd give him that.

I could tell he was deteriorating. I could see it in the way he looked and acted. He rested for longer periods of time, he was constantly sick, and he struggled to keep anything down, even his meds. Was he in much pain? Did he think about dying? These were the things that ran through my head that I couldn't ask him.

If it were me, I'd be thinking about it all the time. Every time I closed my eyes I'd be wondering if I would be waking up. I admired his strength, and his ability to keep positive, because even though time kept creeping, by Andy kept on fighting.

"So," I asked, reaching across the table for the milk. Andy sat opposite me, flicking through the paper. It was Wednesday morning, and I was waiting to see what the day was going to hold. "Do we get to see this list?" I wondered what else he had on there. This whole experience had me thinking about my own mortality, and what I wanted to achieve in life.

"Nope. Much more fun for me if you guys don't know what's coming next," Andy said with a grin. Marta placed a handful of pills in front of him. "I think you'll enjoy today, though, man," he said, arranging the pills in front of him by size.

"Are you going to take them or play with them?" I asked, nodding in front of him.

He rolled his eyes and threw one in his mouth, followed by a sip of water, gagging on the liquid. *He can barely swallow.* I looked over at Marta to see if she'd been watching. Her eyes met mine as she gave me a sympathetic smile. What did this mean? Things were getting worse . . . so what was next? It was weird, but I felt so underprepared. I didn't know what to expect when it came to his final days. The whole idea of watching him go through that scared the hell out of me, especially when I kept telling myself that we still had time.

"What about me?" asked Em, walking over to the table with two steaming mugs in her hands. "Will I enjoy it?"

She passed Andy his mug of tea and handed me my coffee. I sighed, pressing my lips together as I took in her appearance. She looked so pretty in her jeans and a fitted, blue sweater, but then again, she always looked beautiful. Her long hair was messed up into a ponytail and she wore little makeup, if any.

I glanced back at Andy and watched him struggle down another pill. I had to hold myself together, if only for her.

"You get a rest today. This one is all Seth's."

I groaned, making out that I was dreading it, but I was actually looking forward to whatever it was. The last week of experiences were things I'd never have done if Andy hadn't pushed me into them, and what did you know? I'd actually enjoyed myself. What I enjoyed the most was the amount of time I got to share with Em and Andy.

"Do I get a hint at least?" I asked, raising an eyebrow.

Andy sighed. "Seriously, you're such a pussy, man. Fine, this is something you've wanted for a long time." My eyes immediately fell on Em and then quickly darted away. *She* was the only thing I longed for, but somehow I didn't think that was on today's agenda. I looked back at Andy, who was staring at me intently. My face flushed. I could just tell he'd caught me looking at Em. I could only imagine what was going through his head.

"I've got no idea. Guess I'll just have to wait." I shrugged.

"Guess you will," he echoed, narrowing his eyes at me.

"Well, I guess I better finish getting ready." I stood up and went to my room, taking my coffee with me. He hadn't realized it, but his words had driven home like a knife through my heart. I'd never have her. No matter what the future held, she was the one thing I wanted that I would never have.

Until now I'd been able to fool myself into believing that there was a tiny shred of hope that things could work out. But I was kidding myself. I needed to move on and forget about her like that, because all I was going to do was ruin our friendship.

"I won't let that happen," I muttered to my reflection in the mirror. She needed me and I was going to be there for her. As a friend. Because losing her meant losing everything.

Grabbing my jacket, I left my room and walked back out into the kitchen. Marta was there, alone. Hesitating, I sat down at the table. There was so much I wanted to ask, but at the same time, so many questions I didn't want the answer to. It all felt so complicated.

"He's getting worse, isn't he?" I finally said.

She nodded. "He should be in the hospital. But he's stubborn."

"Is he in much pain?" I asked, not being able to stand the thought of my best friend suffering.

"He's having trouble getting his pain meds down. Even with them, the pain would be significant."

I had one more question, but I couldn't bring myself to say the words. In the back of my mind, I thought about Deb and Karl every day. I vowed that the second he deteriorated, I'd call them. But how would I know when the time was right? What if I completely fucked everything up?

"Is there something you can do? Get a doctor here or

something?" I asked.

"He doesn't want that yet. The doctor can prescribe intravenous pain meds, but it will knock him out. He's not ready for that yet."

"How long?" I finally asked. A lump formed in my throat as I waited for her to answer. I couldn't bring myself to say the words "until he dies."

"A week or so. Maybe more. Maybe less."

I nodded, trying to process the information. A week. One week. Seven days, and my best friend in the world would be gone. It didn't feel real. He had such a presence that imagining him no longer there was impossible.

"They said he had a month at least," I said, my voice hoarse.

"You can never tell for sure how the body is going to behave." Marta patted my hand sympathetically. "Just be there for him, Seth. Be his friend."

***

"NASCAR racing?" I turned to Andy. Was he fucking *kidding* me? This was fucking awesome. I had pushed my earlier conversation with Marta out of my head.

I was determined to make this week memorable.

He laughed and nodded. "Remember when we were nine, how obsessed we were with NASCAR? You begged your parents for that remote-control car for your birthday, and then your dad ran over it a week later."

I laughed. "God, yeah. And then we got those old TV boxes and put together our own cars and sold tickets to the big race."

"You're kidding," Emily sniggered, her pretty blue eyes twinkling at me. "And people actually paid for that?"

"A buck a ticket, you bet they did," Andy said. "Only the night before, we left our cars outside. We didn't realize it was going to rain all night. The next morning, our cars were ruined and we had to give back the fifty-six dollars we'd made."

"You sold fifty-six tickets?" She giggled.

"Yes, we were quite the little salesmen." I laughed. "Or at least Andy was."

He had a knack of being able to convince anyone to do anything, which was one of the reasons he would've made a great lawyer. In the third grade, he convinced the entire class that wearing socks to bed would make your feet fall off. Deb had gotten a lot of angry calls from parents that weekend.

"So what exactly are we doing here?" Excitement began to build inside of me. I had a pretty good idea, but I needed to hear him say it.

"Three laps. You have three laps in Number Twenty over there." I followed his gaze to the revved-up red Chevrolet sitting on the track. My palms began to sweat as I realized this was about to become a reality.

"Holy fuck, man. You're shitting me." This had to be a joke, because it was just way to cool to be real.

"If I can't do it, then you're the next best thing." He shrugged. I felt a pang of sadness. This was his dream as much as it was mine, and it sucked that he had to sit back and watch.

"Come with me," I said, a smile spreading across my lips. He might not be able to drive, but what was stopping him from sitting in that seat next to me as I tore up this track? The worst that could happen would be some pretty serious vomiting, and let's face it, that was a regular occurrence now anyway.

He raised his eyebrows and nodded as though he hadn't thought of that. "Why not?" he murmured, a grin spreading across his lips.

"Are you sure that's a good idea?" Em asked, her voice uncertain. She shot me a look, her eyes wide with fear.

"What's the harm?" I shrugged. "I'll look after him. I promise," I said reassuringly. She nodded, still not looking convinced, but she also knew how much this meant to him.

"Okay," she agreed. "Let's do this, then."

After much convincing of the team in charge, they finally cleared Andy to ride in the car with me. Our instructor ran through some safety precautions and gave me a list of dos and don'ts. I nodded, only half listening because I was so eager to get in and start driving.

"So," he said, finally done with his spiel, "any questions?"

"Nope. I think we're good." I grinned.

He handed me the keys. "Then have fun, and try not to total the car."

I helped Andy into his seat and strapped him in. Em, who was on standby, wheeled his chair away. Climbing into the driver's seat, I felt the blood pumping through my veins. *This is really happening.* I slipped the key into the ignition and started her up.

The wheel shook against my grip, the full power of the machine vibrating through my body. I flashed Andy a grin.

"Are you ready?" I asked.

"Let's do this."

Slamming my foot down on the accelerator, I tore off down the track. I swerved into the first corner as the wheels spun, trying to regain control.

"Yeah!" Andy screamed. He threw his head back and laughed. Slamming my foot down on the pedal again, I screeched through the next turn.

Three laps went by in no time at all. After it was over, I steered the car to the gates. My blood was still pumping as I turned off the ignition and laughed, hitting the palm of my hand against the steering wheel.

"That was . . . holy shit, man." Andy threw his head back and laughed. I smiled, feeling the exact same way, as I ran my hand through my hair. I glanced at Andy, who was looking a little green.

"You look like you're going to hurl." I chuckled. "Maybe you should open the door?"

"Nah, man. I'm fine, I'm just . . ." He shook his head, his smile now even wider. "Fucking wow."

I climbed out of the driver's seat, a little unsteady on my feet. We'd reached a top speed of two hundred and three miles an hour. Leaning against the car as Em steered Andy's seat over, I struggled to catch my breath.

"You look wrecked. I can only imagine how Andy is," she grumbled.

"Relax, he's fine. That's probably the most fun he'll ever have," I snapped. Sighing, I took a step toward her. "I didn't mean it like that. He had fun, so let him enjoy it, okay?"

"I'm just worried, Seth. He's getting worse. I see it every day—"

"Are you planning on helping me out?" Andy's voice cut in as he banged on the window.

"Go help him," I said, squeezing her hand.

Chapter Eleven

Emily

I was worried about him. All this activity was taking its toll. But there was no point asking him to slow down, because he wouldn't. Watching him and Seth race around that track was amazing, and it was obvious how much the experience had meant to him. I was only just beginning to realize just how important doing this with Seth and I was to him.

Today had been the happiest I'd seen him in ages, but it had come at a cost: he'd been sleeping since we got home. Every now and then he would moan like he was in pain, but not wake.

My stomach was a tangle of knots. I was getting closer

and closer to losing him; I knew that. Every change, no matter how tiny, I noticed and obsessed over, wondering what was next. I so badly wanted to freeze time and stop this from happening. I wasn't ready to let him go.

Creeping up from the armchair that sat next to his bed, I leaned over and kissed him gently on the cheek. He stirred, but didn't wake. Quietly I left the room, tiptoeing across the polished wooden floor, closing the door behind me.

Seth had gone out—I didn't know where—and Marta had gone home for a few hours so I had the house to myself. I made myself a cup of coffee and curled up on the sofa with my notebook.

Good memories. I forced myself to write one every day. Because I knew how heavily I was going to rely on them after he was gone.

Pulling a thick mink blanket over my lap, I opened my notebook to a blank page and began to write.

Valentine's Day, 2005. Our first Valentine's together.

I trawled through the offerings in the bookstore at the mall. My heart sank. Nothing seemed right. What do you give to someone who was facing the fight of his life?

A book seemed too impersonal. Chocolates were too

cheap. A teddy bear? Nothing was memorable enough. I groaned in frustration.

"Still nothing?" Seth rounded the corner, raising his eyebrows at me.

"No. I can't think of anything," I grumbled. "You're so lucky you don't have a girlfriend. At least you don't have to worry about all this Valentine's Day shit."

"Yeah," Seth murmured, a sparkle in his eyes. "I'm so lucky."

I grabbed his arm and dragged him out of the store. I was just about ready to give up. A sweater? No, I might as well just give him a pair of freaking socks.

"Em," Seth said with a laugh. "Whatever you give him, he'll love."

"But I want it to be special. It's our first Valentine's together." And maybe our last.

"So make it special." He waved his arms around. "You don't need all this shit to make it special. All you need is you."

My heart swelled. He always knew the right thing to say to me. And he'd just given me the best idea. I stepped forward and hugged him tightly.

"You're the best. Thank you!" I ran off before he could answer.

***

"Wow," Andy mumbled, his eyes widening. He stood in the doorway, staring at me. I blushed, my fingers running over the soft lace of the black, low-cut dress I was wearing. Wait until he saw what was underneath.

He held out a bouquet of roses.

"I didn't know what to get you," he mumbled, his face coloring.

I smiled, taking the roses in my hands and lifting them to my face. I sighed as I breathed in their sweet scent. "They're perfect." I smiled. "Come in."

He followed me inside.

"Whatever you're cooking smells amazing."

"I hope you like slow-cooked beef cheeks." I walked into the kitchen, aware of him following behind me. As I leaned against the counter, he pressed himself up against me.

"I like you more," he mumbled, his lips brushing past my neck. I sighed as his tongue worked its way down to my collarbone. Reaching for my hand, he turned me around.

"Do we have time before dinner?" he asked.

"For what?" I giggled.

"Dessert," he replied, wiggling his eyebrows.

Laughing, I swatted his arm. "You're such a dork."

"Maybe, but I'm your dork." He lifted his hand to my face, resting my jaw against his palm.

I closed my eyes and smiled, amazed at what his touch was capable of doing to me. "It's slow-cooked beef," I said. "It can cook all night if it has to."

I gasped as he lifted me into his arms and carried me off into the bedroom. He set me down and I perched myself on the edge of the bed, gazing up at him. He was so damn sexy, especially the way he was smirking down at me—like he knew something I didn't.

He lifted his shirt over his head and I ran my hands over his bare chest. His skin was so soft and smooth against my fingers. After two rounds of chemo, his hair was beginning to grow back. He looked healthy. He looked like the Andy I knew.

My hands found their way to his belt. I kept my eyes firmly on his as I began to unclasp it, then the buttons. He smiled as I reached inside his boxer shorts and closed my fist around his cock.

"Look at you," he mumbled. He closed his eyes and gasped as I freed his length.

"What about me?" I asked playfully, my fingers stroking his erection. "Do you want me to stop?"

"God, no," he moaned. I pushed his pants down over his hips, letting them pool at his feet. Stepping out of them, he kicked them aside. "Stand up."

He took my hand and pulled me to my feet. His eyes connected with mine as he slipped a hand around the back of my neck and pulled me against him. I sighed as he kissed me, his lips soft and warm against mine.

He tugged at the bottom of my dress, lifting it up and over my arms. I shivered as he stepped back, staring at me, his expression one of awe. I pushed my body against him, my hands circling around his neck as I kissed him...

Seth had been right. I didn't need to spend time and money finding the perfect gift because I was all Andy wanted. And he had me that night, over and over again in various locations around my apartment.

I smiled at the memory, pulling my lip between my teeth. That had been one hell of a night. And I'd learned something: it's not the material things that show a person how much you love them, it's the actions—what you do, how you act, and what you say—that matter.

Chapter Twelve

Seth

Andy didn't get out of bed the next day. Or the day after that. He wasn't doing well, and Em was becoming more upset by the minute. She refused to leave his side, even just to eat or sleep. I had to do something, because sitting by and watching her fall apart wasn't an option.

By Sunday, I insisted Emily come out with me. I just wanted to get her away from the house. She was just going to sit there any worry when there was nothing she could do.

"Where are we going?" she asked, a twinge of annoyance in her voice, finally giving in.

"I don't know, Em. I just wanted to get you out of the

house for a while. What do you want to do?" I asked, sliding the gear stick into drive.

Emily shrugged. Her mind was still on Andy, and no amount of distracting was going to change that.

"He'll be fine."

She nodded, not looking convinced. She bit her lip, gazing out the window. I didn't want Emily to know, but I was worried too. What if something happened to him while we were out? I glanced over at her. Marta was looking after him, but what if he died and we weren't there for him? God, if something happened when I'd all but forced her out of the house . . .

"How about we get some lunch and take it back to the house? We can spend the day lazing on the beach." My hands gripped the steering wheel as I glanced at her. I could try and keep her mind off things while still staying close to home.

"I like that idea," she said, her face softening. "And maybe he'll feel up to joining us later?"

I nodded, swallowing the lump in my throat.

I hope he won't be well enough to join us.

Because spending the whole day with Em was both

terrifying and exciting. My jaw clenched as I realized what I was thinking. I didn't deserve a friend like him. Who thinks that way about someone they're supposed to care about, especially when they're *dying*?

I cringed as I remembered our conversation from the other day. He knew. He knew how I felt about her. And more than that, he didn't hate me for it. It was almost like he understood. But I still couldn't figure out why he'd brought it up. What was the point in confronting me about it? Was he worried I would try something? I felt a pang of anger that he'd think I was capable of that. I'd never risk losing her friendship, no matter how in love with her I was.

You need to let her go. Loving her is going to rip you apart.

I wanted to laugh. Because how could the way I felt possibly be a negative thing? It just wasn't right. I loved her so fucking much, and I couldn't do a damn thing about it. She would never know that someone out there loved her just as much as Andy did.

"Seth?"

I felt the color rise to my cheeks. Breaking out of my own head, I focused on Em. She was looking at me, waiting for me to say something.

"I'm sorry, what?"

"I asked if you think we're doing the right thing, keeping this from Deb and Karl? I mean, how will we know when to call them? I can't imagine if . . ." She broke off.

I swallowed hard. I'd been thinking that too. What if they never got the chance to say goodbye? "I don't know, Em." And I didn't. I had no fucking idea about any of this shit. I was sick of everything. I was sick of second guessing my every action, wondering if I was doing the right thing. I hated feeling helpless.

**

We grabbed some sandwiches from the deli in town and some supplies from the grocer's, and headed back to the house. It was just after noon and the sun was out, making it the perfect day to be spending outside.

I carried the bags into the kitchen while Emily went to check on Andy. She came back a few minutes later looking flustered.

"Is he okay?" I asked, my head immediately going to the worst-case scenario: I'd forced her out of the house and now he was dead.

"Yeah, h-he's fine. He was awake." She hesitated. "It's just . . . he snapped at me, told me he wanted some time alone. He's never wanted that before," she said softly.

I put my arm across her body and pulled her against me, my arms curling around her waist. I closed my eyes, my nose buried in her hair, my head engulfed by the sweet smell of her shampoo.

"Don't take it personally, Em. He's allowed to have bad days. If it were me, every day would be bad. Give him some space, and he'll come around." *Only he was running out of time.*

Anxiety began to consume me. Was it a coincidence that he was acting like this after finding out how I felt? Was he punishing *her* for my feelings?

Andy, what the fuck are you doing?

He thought that by pushing her away, he could spare her the pain. Only it was too late for that. What he was doing was only going to make things worse.

"You take these out," I said, handing her our lunch. "I'm just going to use the bathroom and I'll bring out some drinks, okay?"

I waited until she'd left and then headed to Andy's

room. He looked up when I entered without knocking.

"What's up?" He lay on the bed in his green flannel pajamas with the covers over the top of him. His eyes were heavy and dark, making his pasty, white skin look even paler.

Fuck, he looks bad. I swallowed, forcing myself to focus on why I'd gone in there. "Emily," I replied, crossing my arms. "I know what you're doing. And all you're going to end up doing is hurting her more."

Andy laughed. "Right. I forgot you're the expert when it comes to my girlfriend."

What the hell did he mean by that? Was *that* was this was about?

"I don't care if you're dying, man. You don't get to punish her. She needs you. She needs this time with you. Don't push her away."

"I'm not, for fuck's sake." He shook his head and closed his eyes. "Did she tell you I shat myself this morning? Or that she had to clean me up because Marta was out getting my medications? Or how my catheter leaked so the whole fucking bed stank of urine? I don't want those to be the memories she's left with." Andy sighed, his face creasing in pain as he struggled to sit up.

I didn't know what to say. I was so caught up in protecting Em from feeling unwanted that my best friend going through his own private hell had somehow become an afterthought.

"I didn't know that," I said quietly. I sat down in the worn, leather armchair, struggling to think of what to say. There was no winner in this conversation: he was dying, she was watching him die, and I was watching her watch him die. We were all suffering. How do you move past that?

"Look, if I feel up to it I'll get up later, okay?" he muttered. "But right now, I can't be around anyone. But you need to be there for her, because she needs someone."

I nodded. "Andy?" He waited for me to continue. "I'm sorry. I know this is hard for you. And I'm sorry for how I feel. I just . . . you have to know I've never acted on it, because you're like a brother to me."

"It's okay, man. I'm not angry." He sighed and shrugged his shoulders, a bitter laugh escaping his mouth. "I love you for being there for her. She's going to need you when I'm gone." He paused, his expression serious. "You know, I'm okay with dying. I've come to terms with that. It's the thought of leaving her that I can't stand."

I nodded, because I got it. I really did.

Chapter Thirteen

Emily

"What do you think happens when we die?" I turned to Seth, my eyes searching his. I didn't want the truth; I wanted comfort. I wanted him to tell me everything was going to be okay.

It was Monday afternoon, and we lay on the deck, staring out at the sea. The gray, overcast sky looked threatening as the waves crashed over the rocks, sending a foamy mess racing along the sandy bank. It was such a beautiful place, but at the same time the formation of the rocks and the way the water collided against them with angry fury was scary. Unpredictable. Kind of like how I was feeling.

Seth breathed out, his face creased, his blue eyes clouding over as he thought about my question. I studied him for a moment. There were so many little details about him that I'd never noticed, like the way his jaw twitched when he was deep in thought, or the way the left side of his mouth rose higher than the right when he smiled. And had that dimple always been there? Because I hadn't noticed how cute it made him look when he laughed. I looked back out at the water.

"I don't know, Em. I think there is something else after all this. I think that we come back and get to start over, and spend our lives looking for that one special person again."

"You think there is only one person for each of us?" I asked softly. The thought made me sad. If that were true, then I'd never know love again. I'd never experience that rush of excitement of new love.

Anger bubbled inside of me. Who cared whether or not it was true? I didn't *want* anyone else. I wanted Andy.

Seth shrugged. "I don't know. But I think we know when something is right. And that's what we look for. The feeling that nobody else in the world can compare. That without this person, your life is worthless, it has no point. I think you can have that more than once in a lifetime."

I nodded numbly. I didn't believe in anything. I'd lost too many people I loved for me to believe that everything happens for a reason. I snuggled closer into Seth's shoulder as I thought about life and living, dying and death. Maybe I was destined to be alone. Losing the people I loved was too painful. Maybe it was easier to shut myself off than to risk going through this all again.

My fingers traced the cover of my notebook, the leather soft and luxurious against my touch. I glanced down and stared at the three words embroidered onto the front. *Hope. Love. Happiness.* I'd thought it was a sign when I saw it in the window of the gift shop. Who knows? Maybe it had been.

Seth glanced at me. "What do you write in that?" he asked. "I never see you without it these days."

I handed it to him. His eyes widened as he took it, staring at it for a moment before flipping it open.

"It was Andy's idea," I explained. "That I write down one happy memory each day, so that when . . . after . . . I'll have all these amazing memories to look back on." I peered over his shoulder to see which one he was reading: the night I passed my final exams. I smiled at the thought.

He chuckled. "I'd forgotten about that night. I think that was the only time I really ever saw you drunk. As in, so drunk you could barely function."

"That's because you and Andy kept refilling my glass. I thought I was on my first wine, when in reality I'd had about ten," I exclaimed. "My memory of that night is surprisingly pretty clear." I giggled.

"So you recall the prank calls then?" He laughed.

I cringed and groaned. Unfortunately I did. He and Andy had gotten me so drunk and then dared me to prank my professor. Which of course I had—ten times—pretending I was in love with him. The worst part was the professor was actually married, and a really nice guy. Or so I'd thought.

"That was your fault," I grumbled, my face heating up at the thought. "You knew I wouldn't be able to turn down a bet."

"I was pretty impressed you were able to pull it off. You actually got him to agree to meet you for sex."

"Don't remind me," I cried, laughing. Not that I would have ever gone through with it, but it did make retrieving my graded assignments off him the next week extremely awkward.

"*That* is why I don't drink. Because I'm too easily influenced by you and Andy."

"Bullshit. You're too competitive, is more like it," he teased, nudging me.

I glowered at him, knowing he was right.

"And then Andy ordered fifty pizzas with extra sausage to be delivered to Professor Walton because he gave him less than a perfect score."

"Oh God, the look on his face when he opened the door," I cried, tears streaming down my face. "And I still can't believe you guys made me hide in the bushes outside his house."

"But it was worth it." Seth chuckled. "I'd never heard him use so many cuss words before." He shook his head, his eyes clouding over. "We had some good times, didn't we?"

I nodded. We had. The best times. When the three of us got together, anything could—and usually did—happen.

"I might just go and check on him," I said, getting up. I walked back inside and made my way to his room. Every time I walked down that hallway a knot formed in my stomach. Seeing him only reminded me how sick he really was.

I pushed open the bedroom door. He was still sleeping. Quietly, I crept around to the side of the bed and pulled back the covers, climbing in next to him. I wrapped my arms around his waist. He stirred, mumbling incoherently. I reached down for the second blanket that lay at the foot of the bed. He was so cold.

Covering him, I gently rubbed along his arms, trying to warm him up. His breathing—shallower and faster than usual—was beginning to sound congested. *I hope he's not getting a cold.*

I laughed bitterly, the irony of my thought hitting me. *He's dying of cancer and I'm worried about him getting a cold.*

The all too familiar pang of anxiety began to consume me. *No. Focus on good thoughts. Do it for him.* Sitting up in the bed, I opened my notebook and began to write.

First day at Delton Middle School, January 2000

Starting a new school halfway through the school year sucked. Especially when the teacher decided it would be all sorts of fun to make you stand at the front of the room and talk about yourself. I was sure she got pleasure out of watching my discomfort.

"Uh, hi," I began, rubbing my sweating palms together. "I'm Emily Callington. We just moved here from Los Angeles. My dad is a police officer and we move around a lot."

Apparently this was where we were settling down. Why did it have to be here, in a town where I knew nobody? What was wrong with L.A., where all my friends were?

I moved to sit down. The teacher put her hand up to stop me.

"Tell us something about you, Emily."

About me? My heart thudded so loudly it was all I could hear as I struggled to think.

"I like the Gilmore Girls, *" I offered, my voice small. The class sniggered. "I also like N*Sync." More laughter. The teacher nodded, excusing me.*

I practically ran to the only vacant seat as the teacher continued with the class. Everyone was staring at me. I slumped down into the corner seat in the back row, my heart sinking. This place sucked. I was going to hate it; I could just tell.

At lunchtime, I sat by myself outside the cafeteria, only

*because eating inside meant eating alone and having
everyone talk about me. At least out here I could pretend I
was invisible. I opened my lunch bag and pulled out my
peanut butter and jelly sandwich.*

"Hey."

*I looked up. Two boys were standing in front of me. I
recognized them from my class. I smiled shyly. What did
they want? Knowing my luck, they were here to make fun of
me. Because I needed my life to be more difficult right now.*

*"I'm Andy." The dark-haired boy flopped down on the
bench opposite me. "That's Seth." I smiled at the other
boy, who smiled back. My heart fluttered as I took in his
light-brown hair and blue eyes. He was cute, and the
awkwardness he had about him made him even cuter.*

"I'm Emily." But they already knew that.

*"You want to hang out with us?" asked Andy. I nodded.
They seemed nice, and it beat eating alone. I gathered up
my lunch and followed them inside.*

*"Over there—they are the kids that think they're better
than everyone. Try to avoid them." Andy glanced around.
"And those kids are the weirdos. That's probably where
you would've ended up if it wasn't for us." He smirked, his*

dark eyes full of humor.

"You two seem pretty weird to me," I shot back. Seth laughed as Andy narrowed his eyes at him.

"What? She's right."

Andy turned back to me. "If you're going to hang out with us, you have to follow a few rules."

I crossed my arms across my chest. Rules? I hated rules.

"Like?" I asked suspiciously.

"Like no talking about the Gilmore Girls, *for starters. I hear enough about that stupid show from my mom. And on Sundays we skateboard down by the beach, so you'll need to do that too. And you better like Xbox."*

"I prefer PlayStation," I said.

I didn't. I didn't even own a video game, but I liked arguing with Andy. It made him angry, and he was cute when he was angry.

He sighed. "Okay, whatever. You want to come over to my house tonight?"

I nodded shyly. "I'll have to check with my mom, but that sounds good."

From that first moment, they'd accepted me. What could

have turned out to be the worst few years of my life had turned into the best because I'd met Seth and Andy. The three of us were inseparable, with every spare minute spent together. I thought I'd had friends in the past, but everything else paled in comparison to the relationship I shared with Seth and Andy.

I closed my book and lay back on the bed, a smile on my face, my fingers tracing along the spine of my notebook. I had so many great childhood memories, all thanks to those two. I often wondered how different things would've been if my parents had decided on a different town, or a different school.

Friendships like ours were rare. They didn't come along often, so when they did you had to make the most of them. The uniqueness of ours was we were like three pieces to a puzzle; it didn't feel right if one was missing.

If I believed in soul mates, then that's what we'd be, all three of us. If I believed things happened for a reason, then I'd believe I was meant to meet them, that our friendship was an unavoidable certainty. But I didn't believe in all that. Because then I'd start to question why all *this* was happening—and what I had done that was so bad that I deserved to lose every person I held dear to me.

And then I'd wonder how long would it be until I lost Seth too.

Chapter Fourteen

Seth

By Thursday afternoon, Andy was feeling well enough to get out of bed for short periods of time which he, of course, took to mean he was well enough to leave the house. Even Marta couldn't convince him to take it easy.

"Maybe you should take another day to rest," Marta suggested. I nodded, thinking exactly the same thing.

"Sorry, guys, but you're not getting out of this one. Besides, everything is all booked."

I groaned and shut my eyes. I didn't even want to know.

"Oh, before I forget." He grinned widely as he handed Em and me each an envelope.

"What is this?" I asked suspiciously.

"Open it and find out."

I slipped my finger along the length of the silver envelope, slitting it open. Inside was a folded piece of paper. I opened it and read.

"You're having a wake?" Em said in disbelief. I snuck a look at her. She looked hurt. And angry. Really angry.

"A live wake." He nodded proudly. "For this Saturday. I've invited all the guys from college, and a few other people. Nothing big, just something I would rather do while I can enjoy it, rather than when I'm in the ground."

I cringed. I hated it when he spoke like that. "Is this on your list?" I asked, skimming the details. My eyes widened as I read the last line. "Fancy dress? Come as your favorite terminal illness? You're *got* to be fucking kidding me, man." I groaned. That was so . . . morbid.

"What?" He chuckled, obviously enjoying my reaction. "Don't you remember all the parties we had in college?"

"The parties *you* had. At our place, while *I* tried to study over the noise," I corrected him. "And yes, I remember. How the hell could I forget you and your fucked up parties?"

"So this shouldn't surprise you, then," he said, winking at me. He turned to Marta. "You're welcome to join us, too."

"I honestly cannot think of a worse way to spend my Saturday night," she replied, her voice sour. Andy rolled his eyes and turned to Em, who had said nothing for the last few minutes. She stood up and walked out of the room.

I wanted to go after her and make sure she was okay, but it felt weird. Andy should be the one checking in on her, not me. I waited until it was obvious he wasn't planning on doing that.

"Dude, I think she's upset," I said.

He shrugged. "So go check on her."

I stared at him, shocked by his indifference. What the hell was going on with him?

"Marta, can you push me out to the deck," he muttered. She nodded and walked around to the back of his chair. I watched as she pushed him outside, then came back in and closed the door behind her.

"What was all that about?" I muttered, more to myself than her.

"The cancer is eating away at him, Seth. These

personality changes are common with late-stage cancer. Go and speak to Emily. Make sure she knows that this isn't about her. It's just the progression of his disease."

I nodded. It made sense. The cancer had changed his physical abilities so much, but it hadn't occurred to me the effect it would be having on his brain. Kicking my chair back, I stood up.

I found Em lying on her bed, staring at the wall, clutching her notebook to her chest. Her face was wet— tear-stained—her dark hair floating freely around her face. I sat down on the bed and reached out, gently swatting aside strands of her hair.

"Em, are you okay?" I asked, my hand resting on her shoulder.

"It's like he's *trying* to make this harder," she whispered. "I feel like he wants to hurt me."

I sat down and scooped her into my arms, sitting her up next to me. "Em, when he's like that it's not Andy talking. Cancer is fucked up and it's not fair. But you've just got to remember that he loves you, and would never do anything to intentionally hurt you."

She smiled, her arms tightening around me. "I know.

And I know it's selfish of me when he's the one dying, but I just don't know what to do anymore. I don't know what to say, or how to act. I just feel like I'm the mess and everyone is trying to hold me together."

"And that's okay," I whispered, kissing her temple. "Because nobody is denying that this is just as hard for you to go through. Andy will die and you'll still be here. The world won't stop moving, even though you might feel your world has. That's an incredibly hard thing to work through."

"When my parents died, it was you and Andy who got me through it. I just don't know if I can do it all over again." She turned to me, her eyes wide with fear. "What if I lose you too?"

I held her close to me, my heart breaking for her. If only she knew how much I loved her, and how I would do anything to make her feel happiness again. I'd give everything for this girl. I'd give my life if it meant seeing her smile.

"I've told you, I'm not going anywhere. You're stuck with me."

Chapter Fifteen

Emily

He was much quieter today. As often as he kept telling me that he was feeling better, I wasn't sure that I believed him. He'd slept nearly the whole half-hour drive to our destination, only waking just as we arrived. I shot Seth a confused look as we pulled up outside a ranch. He just shrugged.

"This the right place?" he asked, peering at Andy through the rearview mirror.

"Yep. Drive down toward that barn," he said. As we continued along the dirt driveway, we passed a sign that read *Stanton's Bulls. Breeders since 1887.* My stomach dropped. *Bulls?*

He was crazy if he thought I was going to get on a bull.

"Andy," I began, biting my lip. "What are we doing at a bull farm?"

"Bull-riding," he said, as if I'd asked the stupidest question in the world.

"No," I said, shaking my head. "Nuh-uh. There's no fucking way are you going to get me on one of them. I don't care how much you guilt-trip me."

"What's wrong?" Seth smirked at me. "You scared?"

My eyes widened. "I'm not scared," I scoffed, scowling at him.

He was really on Andy's side right now? Of course he was. I could see how much Seth had been enjoying the last few days. He and Andy were so similar in many ways, and living out this list was like his own dreams come true. I, on the other hand, would not have put bull-riding on my bucket list, even if I had to name a thousand things.

"I just don't feel like getting rammed into the dirt by a pissed-off bull."

"Come on, Em. If you're chicken, it's okay. We'll understand, won't we?" Andy said, joining in.

I knew what they were doing, and as much as I didn't want it to work, it was. If there was one thing I hated, it was people thinking I was scared. Andy and Seth had been doing this for eleven years to get me to do what they wanted. They knew exactly how to push my buttons. And they knew I'd cave in order to prove myself.

"Fine," I shot back, ignoring the grin they exchanged. "And you can stop looking so damn cocky. You're both assholes."

They laughed hysterically, which only made me more annoyed. I was glad I could be such a source of amusement for them.

"You make it so easy," teased Seth. "We shouldn't enjoy it, but God, Em." He shook his head. "Messing with you is just so much fun." I glowered at him as he pulled up outside the barn.

"Eat me," I muttered, sticking my tongue out. Opening the car door, I climbed out, slamming the door shut, their laughter still ringing in my ears. "And you can get your own damn chair," I said to Andy as he opened his door.

"Oh come on, Em. Don't be like that. We're just having fun with you." He reached for my hand, his fingers entwining with mine. How could I stay mad at him?

Especially with those damn deep-brown eyes melting in front of me. He had this way of always making me forgive him, and I hated it.

I softened, relaxing against his touch. He grinned. He knew he had me.

"Fine," I mumbled. "Let's just get this over with."

"I promise you'll have fun," he assured me. Fun? I doubted it.

***

Okay, so maybe I was having a *little* bit of fun.

Who knew trying to sit atop an out-of-control and angry twelve-hundred-pound animal could be so much fun? The best part was that I was beating Seth. After an intensive training session to master the basics, I was pretty stoked with my 2.045 seconds on top of my bull.

"Ha, suck that, Walkerson," I said triumphantly as I hobbled to the edge of the ring. I could barely walk, but it was worth it to see the excitement on Andy's face.

Seth rolled his eyes as he sat on top of his bull. "You're not a nice person when you get competitive," he joked. He patted the neck of his beast. "Let's show her how this is done, Randy."

I giggled uncontrollably as his bull bolted into the ring, bucking him off immediately. "That's how it's done?" I asked innocently.

"Nobody likes a show-off." He stood up and brushed himself off as Andy and I sniggered. "How did I do, Tony?" he asked our trainer.

Tony smirked. "0.874 seconds."

"Ha! I did it," I said, breaking into a dance. Seth rolled his eyes, but I could see how proud he was of me. "Are you impressed?" I asked Andy. I walked over and kissed him as he smiled at me.

"Very," he admitted. "I thought Seth would kick your ass." His hand whipped around behind me, slapping me gently on the butt. "Hey," he said, catching my playful glare. "I was rooting for you."

"Well that's okay then," I grinned.

***

Instead of going home where Andy obviously needed to be, we were headed into the town to find a tattoo parlor. He'd gotten worse since we left the ranch. Every breath was accompanied by him gasping to control the pain, but he refused to do anything Seth or I said.

"There," Andy said. I looked out my window and saw the tattoo place he was pointing to. "Go around the block. There was a parking spot out front."

"Let's just go home. Nobody in his or her right mind is going to do this to you. Look at you. You can barely breathe."

As if on cue, he exhaled sharply, his body shuddering. "Have you seen the kinds of people in these joints?" Andy joked, managing a chuckle. "Trust me, they aren't going to have a problem doing this."

The young guy in the shop, heavily tattooed and pierced, raised his eyebrows as we walked in. The place was empty, apart from the dude and a girl laying on her stomach on one of the beds. Ink went in all directions across her back like a rainbow.

"Can I help you?" the guy asked, getting up off his chair.

Andy nodded confidently. "Yes, I think you can. I'm looking for a tattoo. Can you fit me in? I'd make an appointment, but I can't promise I'll still be alive to honor it."

The guy's eyes widened. He glanced back at the girl he'd been working on, who shrugged. "What were you looking for?" He patted the second bed. "Can you get up here okay?" he asked, his voice uncertain.

Seth wheeled Andy over and helped him out of his chair. I stood back, my arms across my chest, taking in the images that donned the walls.

Tattoos were something that had never interested me, and I was surprised that Andy wanted one. He'd never mentioned it before today. The whole concept of injecting ink into my skin wasn't something I found particularly appealing.

"What were you looking for?" he asked again.

Andy lifted up his shirt. "Just a little something on my back."

"Did you have a design in mind?"

"I do." Andy grinned as he reached into his pocket and pulled out a crumpled bit of paper. "Don't tell them. I want it to be a surprise."

The guy took the paper and smoothed it out. He began to laugh. "Are you serious?" he said with a grin. "Because I will totally do this."

"Dead serious," Andy shot back, his eyes twinkling.

"Man, what are you doing?" Seth groaned, shaking his head.

"What, are you going to tell me to think about it, that it's permanent? That it will be with me for the rest of my life?"

Seth shot him a dirty look. "Just don't do anything that is going to get us killed by your mother, okay?"

"Well don't let her flip me over and she'll never know." He turned back to the guy. "Is this going to hurt?"

"Um, yeah," he replied, his eyebrows shooting up.

Andy shrugged, and then nodded. "Great. Maybe it will take my mind off the crushing pain in my chest."

I covered my face with my hands; I couldn't help it. This whole thing made me want to laugh. Seth was eyeing me like I was crazy, and maybe I was, but this guy was just so cool with Andy's insane behavior that it was hysterical.

"Are you laughing, Emsky?" Andy accused.

My body shook as big chuckles escaped from my lips. "I'm sorry," I gasped, "but this is just so freaking crazy . . ." I walked over to watch the guy at work.

"Hey, no peeking!" Andy yelled.

I ignored him and looked at his back as the tattooist began to poke black ink along the outline of the words he had written. I chuckled even harder. Seth jumped up and came to my side.

"If you're watching then so am I." His brows furrowed, and then he laughed. "Are you kidding me? You mom is going to freak."

Right across the center of his back, in big bold letters, were the words

Fuck you Cancer! It filled half of his back.

"Doesn't that hurt?" I winced. Fuck, I was in pain just watching him.

"Actually, no. I think most of the nerves in my back are shot. If you're ever going to get a tattoo, do it when you're dying," he grinned.

I walked away, pretending I was looking at the designs on the wall. Really, his words had gotten to me. I wiped my eyes, embarrassed that my emotions were getting to me.

It was rare, but sometimes I actually managed to forget that he was dying. And then I'd remember. And my world would come crashing down again. This was one of those times.

"All done." Andy turned, proudly showing off his new artwork. I had to laugh, because all I could see in my head was Deb's face when she saw that. "Okay, now we can go home."

"Not just yet," I said in my most mysterious voice. Andy's brow creased as I walked over to the tattooist. "Can you write Andy here?" I asked, pointing to the inside of my wrist.

"Sure. Take a seat."

"Em," Andy said, his eyes widening. "No way."

"Why not?" I argued. "You did. This way I can remember you."

He opened his mouth to say something else, but thought better of it. "I love you so fucking much," he whispered, love in his eyes. He sat next to me for the twenty minutes it took to have his name forever engraved into my skin. When it was finished, I held it up, examining my swollen red and blotchy skin and the beautifully scrawled *Andy* in the center of it.

"The swelling will go down after a few days, just rub some of this on it twice a day and keep it covered until it dries out." He handed me a small bottle of cream.

"Anything for you?" he asked Seth.

"Hell, no." He turned to Andy. "You know I love you dude, but not happening."

I chuckled as we walked out, holding my throbbing wrist in my hand. *I can't believe I actually did that.* Andy had promised I'd enjoy myself, and while I'd been doubtful, I had to admit that he had been right. Thanks to him, I was pushing myself to experience things I never would've even considered had it not been for him.

***

I lay on the bed just watching him. Even asleep, he sounded awful; his chest was so congested that every inhale sounded like he had a lake in his lungs. Cora, my boss, had told me that as the lungs began to shut down it would become harder and harder for him to breathe.

Reaching out, I stroked his hair. It had grown back lighter than before and was fine like baby hair. I looked up as Marta poked her head in the door.

"How is he?" she asked softly.

I shrugged, tears pricking my eyes. "He sounds horrible," I whispered. My lip trembled as it became harder to hold back the wave of emotion that was waiting to release.

"He should be in the hospital. Or at the very least, he needs a doctor."

I nodded, knowing that as well as she did. The hospital wasn't what he wanted, though. There was no getting better from this, and I was determined to honor his wishes for as long as I could. But I couldn't stand to see him in pain.

"Can you call a doctor? Do you know someone?" I asked. We were hours away from home and his medical team.

She nodded, giving me a sympathetic smile as she backed out of the room.

I turned back to Andy and took his hand, folding my fingers between his. Carefully, I unwrapped the bandage that had been neatly wrapped around my tattoo. It was red and angry, but seeing his name etched onto me made me smile. It had been a small gesture, but this was my way of remembering him.

Chapter Sixteen

Seth

Where the hell am I supposed to get half this shit from?

It was Friday afternoon and I was at the Home Depot with a list of supplies Andy had given me for the wake. The whole idea of a live wake still irked me, but there was no talking him out of it. Marta had told me it was pretty common for those who were dying to want to say goodbye. I understood that, but calling it a wake seemed so morbid. But that was Andy: he wanted to be remembered.

He and Em were spending the day together, and for once I'd felt like a third wheel, which was why I'd jumped at the chance to do his last-minute shopping. Watching the two of them together was hard, especially when he was so sick. I could see how much he loved her, and I could see how much she was hurting. I so badly wanted to be the one comforting her.

I left Home Depot with everything Andy had asked for. It was still pretty early, and I wasn't ready to head back home just yet. I spied a Starbucks across the road and made my way over.

Sitting down with my coffee, I pulled out my phone just as it began to ring. My heart sank as the name flashed across the screen. It was Deb. She hadn't called for a couple of days. I felt so bad about lying to her. She had to be freaking out; her son was dying, and she had no idea where he was. How was that fair?

Before I realized what I was doing, I'd pressed answer. I held the phone to my ear and struggled to think of words to say that would make up for this.

"Seth? Is that you? God, please tell me he's okay." Deb's voice broke as she began to cry.

My heart pounded. I was angry at myself, and angry at Andy for putting me in this position. "Deb, he's okay. I'm sorry, he begged us to take him . . . I'm sorry." Who cared if I was sorry? It didn't fix things. It didn't give her more time with her son.

"How is he?" She wept.

"He's deteriorated. Some days he's better than others." It felt odd saying that, considering he didn't have very long left. Somehow, I knew the better days were behind him now. I could only see things getting worse from here, but I didn't want Deb driving upset.

"Oh, God."

"He has a nurse looking after him, but he really needs more." I hesitated. "He needs a doctor, or a hospital, but he won't. You know how stubborn he is."

"Please tell me where you are, Seth. Please, I need to see him. I need to say goodbye."

I closed my eyes. I so badly wanted to keep my promise to him, but if he died without Deb getting the chance to say farewell, I'd never forgive myself. I had no idea what to do.

"Please, Seth. I'm begging you," she pleaded.

"Millicent Beach," I mumbled. "22 Standbury Lane. He's having a wake tomorrow." I didn't mention it was fancy dress.

"A wake?" She gasped. "Oh, God, thank you, Seth. Thank you so, so much."

I hung up. Had I done the right thing? He would

probably hate me, but no more than I'd hate myself if I hadn't told her. I glanced at my watch. It was nearly six in the evening. She wouldn't get here until tomorrow afternoon, even if she left now.

There was no point in telling him today.

***

As I walked through the kitchen, I saw Em lying down out on the deck. Grabbing two sodas, I went out. She looked up as I approached. She smiled, her eyes red and swollen.

"How is he?" I asked.

"Not great." She reached for the soda I held out to her and set it down beside her. "He finally let Marta call for a doctor."

I sat down on the edge of the bed, staring at the unopened can in my hands. That meant things were bad.

"Are you okay?" I said.

She shuffled over as I climbed onto the cream-colored frilly cushion beside her. *Of course she isn't okay.* I closed my arms around her as she sobbed into my chest. My fingers gently stroked her hair as my lips brushed over her forehead.

***

We stayed out on the deck for the next hour. She had fallen asleep, and I didn't want to wake her because I knew that she hadn't been sleeping well. I studied her face. Her eyes were closed, the faintest of smiles present on her lips. Was she dreaming about Andy? Whatever it was, at least for a moment she would be happy.

I glanced inside. I could see Marta talking to a man in the kitchen. The doctor? It had to be. My stomach tightened. Things must be bad for Andy to have let her call the doctor. If anything, at least I felt as though I'd made the right decision in telling Deb. I just hoped she got here in time.

Em stirred and then rolled over. I gently eased my arm out from under her, covering her with a blanket. She snored softly and snuggled into the warmth. I stood up, careful not to wake her, and crept over to the door. Easing it open, I walked inside. Marta and the man both looked up.

"How is she?" Marta asked.

"Exhausted. Upset. About what you'd expect. How's Andy?"

The look they exchanged said it all. *That bad.*

"All we can do is make him comfortable," Marta finally said. "This is Mike Alson. He's a doctor in town. You . . . might want to call his family, Seth."

"They're already on their way," I said. My mouth felt numb, like the words were sticking to them as I tried to force them out. "I might go check on him, if that's okay."

"Of course," she said. "He's on morphine for the pain now. He might be pretty out of it."

Walking into his room, I wasn't prepared for just how bad he was. I sat down next to the bed and reached for his hand. He was so pale. Huge dark circles surrounded his eyes, and his cheeks were beginning to hollow.

At least he looks comfortable.

This was really happening: Andy was dying. There was no magical cure that was going to save him. He wasn't going to get better. His time was up, whether we were ready to accept that or not.

I sat there, holding his hand until he suddenly squeezed it. My eyes jerked open and I saw him looking at me. *Shit, I must have fallen asleep.*

"Hey man. You're awake," I said, sitting forward.

He tried to smile, but ended up having a coughing fit.

"You need to look after her," he mumbled. He could barely keep his eyes open, the call of sleep was so strong.

"Of course I will."

"No, I want to know you'll be there for her. Really be there for her. Don't make me say it, man."

"She doesn't want me like that. It's you that she loves. And you're dying."

"No, please, Seth. I need to know she will be okay," he mumbled.

"I'll look out for her. You know I'll be there for her."

Chapter Seventeen

Emily

I knocked lightly on the door. Seth looked up as I walked in and smiled. I forced a smile back. Andy was sleeping, just as he had been all day. The morphine really knocked him around. When he was awake, he was delusional and confused. One moment I'd think he didn't even recognize me, and the next he'd say something that convinced me he did.

Seth stood up, kissing me on the head as he walked past.

"I'll be out there if you need me." I waited until he had walked out before I made my way over to the bed. As I sat down, his eyes fluttered open. He stretched his fingers out, wrapping them around my hand. I smiled, blinking back tears.

"Sorry I snapped earlier," he mumbled.

I crawled onto the bed and into his arms, desperate to be as close to him as I could.

"It's okay." I closed my eyes and let him hold me. The feel of his fingers gently stroking my bare skin was almost enough to make me cry. I'd miss this the most.

Lying in his arms, his body up against mine, I took in the sound of each shallow breath. His skin was cold and clammy. I snuggled against him, trying to warm his body. Tears pricked my eyes. I wiped them away as they began to roll down my cheeks.

"Em," he whispered in my ear, pulling me closer to him. "Don't cry. I hate seeing you upset."

"I'm sorry, I just . . ." There was nothing for me to say.

He kissed my cheek, his soft voice soothing me as he held me. "I'll always be with you, Emsky. No matter where you are, or what you're doing, I'll be right there with you."

"I don't want to do anything without you."

He chuckled softly. "Em, the world doesn't stop turning just because I'm not in it."

"My world does," I whispered.

He kissed my cheek. "Come here," he said.

I did, collapsing into his arms as they wrapped around me.

"You need to stop this. *You* aren't dying, Em. You have to promise me that you won't stop living just because I'm gone."

I didn't answer. He didn't want me to give up, but I wasn't sure if I could make that promise to him. I sighed and closed my eyes, pretending we were back home.

"You'll never be alone, Em. Seth will always be there for you."

"I know. But it's not the same."

"Why not?"

"Because I don't love him like I love you."

"He loves you." He spoke softly, his words so gentle they almost floated past me unheard. Almost.

"I love him too—"

"No," he muttered, "He really loves you. He's been loving you for eleven years. Every day, just like I have . . ." He had drifted off again. Placing my hand on his chest, I watched it rise and fall. What was he talking about? Seth wasn't in love with me. I would've picked up on that.

He's just confused. There was no way that could be true.

"Come on Andy, stop messing with me." I pressed my lips together, studying his face for a reaction.

And then I saw it: the way his eyes wouldn't meet mine. It was only for a brief moment, but it was long enough for me to realize it wasn't a lie. I laughed and shook my head. This couldn't be happening. I turned and ran out onto the deck, bolting down the stairs and out toward the beach.

"Em, wait!" Andy's voice carried through the house.

I ignored him and kept running, because I couldn't handle this right now. My boyfriend was dying, and his best friend—*my* best friend—was in *love* with me? This wasn't fair.

I was so angry with both of them, and I was angry with myself. Because deep down, no matter how much I wanted to ignore it, there was a part of me that was in love with him too.

Chapter Eighteen

Emily

He's in love with me.

I felt so deceived. Like our whole friendship was based on one big lie. How could he have not told me that he was in love with me? And for such a long time?

I slowly began to piece together the last fourteen years. Every little action, every word spoken, had it meant something more than I thought it had? I pulled out my notebook. Wiping away tears, I opened it and began to read, desperate for any kind of positivity right now.

Homecoming dance, September, 2005

We hadn't intended on going to the dance, because

dancing sucked. Instead, we had an exciting night planned full of horror movies, popcorn, and Seth's big-screen TV— until Seth's mother insisted he take Cheryl Barmosh, the daughter of one of her friends, who had been dumped by her boyfriend the night before.

So suddenly I had a date with Andy, and nothing to wear. I sat down on my bed, almost in tears. The worst part was I had nobody to talk about this stuff with. Four years ago I wished my mom would stay out of my life. Now, I'd have done anything to have her back.

I think part of the reason I avoided things like dating, dances, and other girly things was because it hurt too much not having her around to share those milestones with.

"Are you okay, sweetie?"

I looked up and saw Deb smiling at me.

"Yeah, I'm just . . ." I broke off as the tears began to fall. She rushed over, her arms wrapping around me. "I have to go to this stupid dance and I have nothing to wear."

"Oh, Em. It's okay. We'll find you something." She stood up, holding out her hand. "Let's go shopping." I smiled and took her hand.

I'd been living with the Graysons since my parents had died. I had no other family, and had it not been for them I would've ended up in foster care. I owed them everything. Deb tried her best to be there for me, but she could never replace my mother, or mend the guilt I still felt over my parents' death.

I stood in front of my mirror, bittersweet emotions racing through me. I couldn't believe the girl staring back at me was actually me. The deep-green chiffon dress highlighted my curves, accentuating my figure. My hair was curled and pinned to the side.

Walking out into the living room, I felt my stomach twist into a bundle of nerves. Andy had never seen me in anything other than a pair of jeans. I wasn't even sure he knew I was a girl. My heart leapt to my throat as he turned around.

His eyes widened as he saw me, his mouth falling open. I blushed at his reaction, secretly pleased that he obviously liked what he saw.

"Wow," he muttered, walking over to me. "Is that you? Holy shit, Em. You look beautiful."

"Thanks," I mumbled, my face red. Deb and Karl stood by the door. She winked at me as we left and I smiled my thanks to her. As we walked out to his car, he took my hand. His fingers weaved between mine, and tingles shot down my spine.

Over the last few weeks, we had been getting closer. I'd convinced myself it was all in my head, that he couldn't possibly see me as anything other than a friend, but the way he was looking at me right now? I wasn't so sure . . .

"We're here," he said, turning off the car. He made no move toward the door; instead, he turned to face me. My heart began to race as he smiled, his lips pressing together. He looked like he wanted to say something. "Do you want to skip the dance?" he asked, his voice soft. Color flushed through his cheeks as he waited for me to respond.

"And do what?" I asked. My gaze dropped. I wasn't sure why I felt so shy all of a sudden.

"We could have dinner. Or go to the beach. Whatever you want," he said.

"Let's go to the beach," I decided. The way I was feeling right then, food was the last thing on my mind.

Satisfied with my decision, Andy start the car and drove away.

We walked along the edge of the water. My shoes dangled freely from my fingers as the waves crashed gently over my toes. Neither of us had spoken since we left the car. I had no idea what he was thinking until he reached for my hand again, his fingers brushing gently over mine.

"Did I mention you look beautiful tonight?"

He stopped, pulling me up against him. I stared into his dark eyes and smiled. Was this really happening? He reached up, his finger brushing aside a stray curl, his eyes never leaving mine.

"I've wanted to do this forever, Em."

"Do what?" I whispered as his lips moved toward me. His hand caressed my chin as he pressed his mouth against mine. My world stopped as he kissed me.

My first kiss.

Seventeen, and my first kiss, and it was with Andy, the boy who had been my rock for the past few years. It was perfect. He pulled away and smiled at me as I wrapped my arms around his neck.

"This is much better than the dance." I giggled. Leaning forward, I pushed my lips against his. He moaned softly as my fingers raked through his thick, curly hair.

"God, Em," he muttered. "I've wanted this for so long. I've wanted you . . . but I didn't think there was a chance. I didn't want to risk our friendship." Hearing him say that made me shiver.

"You should have said something." I giggled. "Because this . . ." I kissed him again. ". . . could've been happening so much sooner."

We spent the next three hours sitting on the beach, exploring each other. It was surreal. I'd known him for so long, yet at that moment I realized there was so much about him I didn't know; so much I wanted to know.

Finally, things were coming together. The universe was on my side for once.

I closed the notebook and kicked off my shoes, crossing my legs up under me. The sand was wet, but I barely noticed. How could such a special memory precede one of the worst moments of my life? Because it was just two weeks later that he was first diagnosed and my world fell apart for the second time.

"Em?"

I stiffened as I looked up and saw Seth approaching. Anger bubbled inside me as I jumped to my feet, my hands balled into tight fists at my side.

"How could you?" I yelled.

"What's wrong? What's happened?" he asked, his expression bewildered.

"Andy told me you're in love with me. Tell me he's lying, Seth. Tell me you wouldn't keep something like that from me."

He dropped his gaze and my heart sank. He couldn't even deny it. I wanted him to laugh, to tell me that was ridiculous. I wanted him to reassure me that nothing was going to change, because him being in love with me changed everything.

"I can't believe this," I mumbled, my hands flying to my head.

"Em—"

"Don't touch me!" I shrieked, jumping back. Had everyone known except me? Maybe I was acting irrationally, but I didn't care. I felt so used.

"What do you want me to say, Em?" He threw his hands up in frustration. "I don't get why you're angry. Is it because I'm in love with you, or because I didn't tell you?" He grabbed hold of my shoulders and forced me to look at him. I stared at him, searching his eyes for the answers to the questions I didn't even know. This changed everything. We could never go back to how we were. How could I look at him in the same way, knowing how he felt about me?

My heart raced as he closed in the space between us. His lips, centimeters from my own, moved toward me and I was frozen; I couldn't move. *He's going to kiss me.*

Holy shit, I *wanted* him to kiss me.

At that moment, there was nothing I wanted more than to feel his lips pressed up against mine. Shivers ran down my spine just thinking about it.

"Just leave me alone," I said, jerking away from him. *I almost let him kiss me.* How could I have done that to Andy?

"Em—"

"Go!" I yelled. I pushed him, watching as he stumbled backwards, shock resonating on his face. Collapsing to my knees, I hugged my arms around me and stared out over the water, refusing to acknowledge what had happened . . . what had almost happened between us.

"Fine," he muttered. He stalked off back in the direction of the beach house. I watched him go, confused by how I was feeling.

Fuck them. Fuck both of them for changing everything.

Chapter Nineteen

Seth

I can't believe he told her.

What the fuck was he doing? My body shook while I stalked across the sand and back into the house, the cold air burning my lungs as I slammed the sliding door shut.

"What do you think you're doing, man?" I asked, storming into his room.

His eyes fluttered open, and he looked at me in confusion. I had woken him, but I didn't feel bad. The only thing I cared about right then was Em and how much she hated me.

"What are you talking about?" he mumbled, rolling over. He winced, his eyes full of pain as he tried to sit up.

155

"Just don't. Stay there," I said, lowering my voice. Taking a deep breath, I tried to calm myself down. Being angry wasn't going to fix anything. I just wanted answers. *What was he doing?*

"What's wrong?" he asked. Then it was like a light bulb went off in his head. He nodded, pressing his lips together. "Em. She told you I told her, didn't she?"

"Why, Andy? Why the fuck would you do that?" I cried, sinking into the armchair. I cradled my head in my hands, trying to figure out a way to make this all better. How could I look after her? How could I be there for he if she wouldn't even look at me?

"She loves you," he said, as if it were that simple. "I've always had a feeling, and these past few days, seeing you two together, I finally realized it."

"You're fucking kidding. That's bullshit."

Andy laughed, anger filling his dark eyes. "You think I want this, man? You think I don't hate myself every day for having this stupid disease? You think I don't hate my body for not being able to fight harder? I do." His gaze fell to the floor. *He can't even stand to look at me.* "But right now I hate you more. Because in a few days, maybe a week, I'll be dead, and it's you who will be there for her."

I shook my head. It didn't make it right. Sure, cancer sucked, and it wasn't fair, but he was messing with the people he was supposed to care about.

"You can't do this, Andy. You can't just play with peoples' feelings and lives just because you're dying. It's not fucking fair." I stormed out of the room.

"Hey, where are you going?" he called after me.

I grabbed my keys and walked out to my car. I didn't know where I was going or what I was doing. I just needed to get away.

***

I drove into town and parked next to the beach. It was raining, but I didn't care. I barely noticed as the thick droplets of water fell down on me. Just when I'd thought things couldn't get anymore fucked up, they had.

I was so angry. Not only at Andy, but at myself, too. Fourteen years was a long time to pine over someone who didn't feel the same way. If I'd just forced myself to move on and forget about her like that, then none of this would be happening right now. But that was the fucking problem: she was all I thought about.

I'd tried moving on. Watching her and Andy together

for all those years was something had almost broken me. I'd been with other girls. I just always ended up back at Em.

Andy's words rolled over in my head. She was in love with *me*? I snorted. Yeah, right. As if I hadn't wished for that every fucking day for the last fourteen years.

Shoving my hands into my pockets, I walked over the bridge and down toward the edge of the water. I sat down on the wet sand, pulling my knees up in front of me and resting my elbows on my knees.

The beach was deserted, no doubt due to a combination of the bad weather and the fact that it was almost dinnertime. Taking my jacket off, I balled it up and placed it behind my head as I lay back and stared up at the sky. I had no desire to go back there anytime soon. Facing Em was something I didn't even want to think about.

She couldn't have feelings for me. No matter how hard I tried to forget his words, I couldn't. They were stuck there in the back of my mind, clouding over my every thought. How did shit get so messed up? I thought back to when we were all just kids: no cares, no worries. Things had been so much easier.

I closed my eyes; I just wanted to forget everything. Just

for a moment. I wanted to be a normal guy who wasn't in love with a woman he could never have, and whose best friend wasn't dying. I shook my head. What was I going to do without him? He had been the center of my life for so long. How was I going to go on without him? I'd spent all my time worrying about how Em was going to cope, but what about me? If I had to be strong for Em, who was going to help me through this? Was our friendship strong enough to survive Andy's death?

Not that it mattered anymore: she hated me. Every time she saw me she would be wondering what my intentions were. We could never go back to the way things were before.

***

I was freezing. I opened my eyes and breathed in sharply, inhaling a mouthful of sand. I coughed and sat up, confused as to why I was passed out on the beach. I looked around me, the only light coming from a nearby dimly-lit streetlight. I struggled to my feet and grabbed my jacket.

Shaking the sand from it, I zipped it up, trying to get some warmth into my body. I walked over to my car and climbed in. The clock shone brightly in the darkness. It was after midnight. I still wasn't ready to go home. I pulled out my phone. A text from Deb sat waiting to be read. Shit. I'd completely forgotten about our earlier conversation.

We are on our way. Please let me know if anything changes. Deb xx

Shoving my phone back in my pocket, I rested my head against the window and closed my eyes. I just wanted to sleep. And maybe when I woke up, things wouldn't be so bad.

Chapter Twenty

Andy

She hadn't left my side all evening. She hadn't spoken either, but in her defense I had been out of it until now. Who knows? Maybe she had been speaking and I just didn't notice?

Pain shot through my body as I repositioned myself to face her. Her head snapped around, her pretty green eyes widening as they locked on mine.

"You're awake," she whispered. Rising from the chair, she sat on the edge of my bed and grasped my hand. Fuck, she was so warm.

"Hey," I mumbled, yawning. Even after sleeping all day,

I was still so, so tired.

"How are you feeling?" she asked. She bit her lip. She did that when she was nervous or stressed. She'd been doing a lot of that lately.

"I'm okay," I said with a little smile. The pain was bad—bad enough that I tried not to breathe in too deeply, or move suddenly—but in a weird way, I liked it. At least I was feeling something. Pain meant I was still alive. The moment that stopped, I would stop. They thought avoiding the IV pain meds was about me trying to be brave, but it was just the opposite. I was terrified to let go.

"Really?" she asked, raising her eyebrows.

I chuckled. There was no fooling her. "Em . . ." I hesitated. "I'm sorry about before. I just so badly want to know you're going to be okay."

Seth was right: I couldn't force two people to be together, no matter how much I wanted it. Most people would probably think it was weird, me trying to hook up my girlfriend and my best friend, but with the exception of me, I couldn't think of anyone who would love her and care for her the way she deserved to be cared for—except him.

Every day I hated myself for leaving her, but if I had to, then I had to make sure she was going to be okay. I couldn't argue that Seth loved her as much as I did. If I wasn't dying, I'd probably kick his ass.

"Don't worry about me," she mumbled, frowning at me. "You've been so focused with pushing me onto Seth that you're not giving me what I so badly need—time with you."

She was right: I was a monster. All I'd done was make things worse for everyone. She climbed into the bed, slipping her head under my arm. I closed my eyes and kissed her forehead, trying to memorize every tiny detail about her. No matter how much my head wanted me to, I couldn't give this up. Still, I needed her to know it was okay for her to move on after I died.

"Em," I began. She looked up at me, her big, green eyes brimming with sadness. I almost lost my nerve. "I want to ask you something."

"Anything," she said.

"We haven't been a proper couple for a long time now. I can't remember the last time I was able to show you how much I love you . . ."

This was coming out all wrong. She looked confused as
hurt filled her eyes. She was probably wondering where the
hell this was going.

I pushed on, determined to get this out. "I think you
have feelings for Seth. I want you to promise me that you'll
let yourself move on after I'm gone."

She shook her head, her eyes hooded with anger. "Stop
this, Andy. Stop it." She struggled out of my arms and sat
on the edge of the bed, her head in her hands. "Why are
you doing this?" She was crying.

"You don't have to tell me, Em. Please," I said reaching
out for her. She pulled away, leaving my empty hand to
collapse on the sheet beside her. "I'm terrified for you, Em.
More than I am for myself. I need to know you'll be okay.
Please . . . I need this."

"You want me to tell you that I'll move on?" she
whispered. She turned around, her eyes red and tearstained.
"Do you have any idea how fucked up and morbid that is?"

I couldn't help but laugh. "Do you know me at all?

Fucked up and morbid is all I know how to do."

In spite of herself, she smiled.

I tried again. "I'm not telling you to move on, Em." I paused, trying to get the words right in my head. "I just need for you to know that it's okay if you do. Seth loves you, and I think you love him. I need you to know that you two being together would make me happy."

"It's . . . I can't even think about that right now." She wept. Her body shook as I reached out and touched her back.

"I love you, Em. I love you so fucking much," I whispered.

She crawled back into my arms and began to cry. I told myself I'd be strong, that I'd never let her see me cry, but there was nothing I could do right then to stop the tears as they rolled down my cheeks.

"I love you too," she whispered, her lips meeting mine. "I'll always love you, Andy. Forever."

"I know you love me, Emsky. I know how much you love me, and without you, I would've lost this battle a long time ago."

"Don't talk like that."

"Why? It's true." I smiled. Her expression turned serious. "Em . . . I don't think it's me that you're in love with anymore." It was the truth. Our relationship hadn't been right for so long now. It had become all about her caring for me.

"What?" She gasped. Hurt filled her eyes. "How can you even think that?"

"Em, I'm sorry. I . . ." I shrugged and wiped my eyes. "I'm sucking at this, aren't I?" All I wanted to do was express to her that it was okay, but everything I said was coming out wrong. "I just want you to be happy."

"My happiness starts and ends with you," she whispered. A single tear rolled down her left cheek. I reached out and wiped it away.

"I don't believe that for a second. You're convincing yourself that you don't deserve to be happy once I'm gone, and that's bullshit."

She curled in closer to me, closing her eyes. "I don't

want to talk about this anymore, Andy. Can we talk about it later?"

I nodded and kissed the top of her head. But I couldn't shake the thought . . . what if there wasn't going to be a later?

***

When I woke up, Em was still curled up in my arms, fast asleep. I smiled at her, lifting my fingers to her face. She didn't stir as I gently traced the outline of her lips. I was going to miss her so much. Dying held no fear at all in comparison to losing her. I'd never kiss those lips again. I'd never feel those arms curl around me, or see the love in her eyes when she looked into mine.

As I reached over to grab my watch and check the time, pain stretched across my chest. It was too much for seven in the morning. I collapsed back against the pillows, struggling for every breath. Was this it? Was I dying? I glanced over at Em. I wasn't ready to leave her.

Just a few more days. Please.

Chapter Twenty-One

Emily

I'm running. Every step I take, I can feel the ice cracking under my feet. Every step, I'm expecting to crash through into the freezing water. I spot Andy standing on the edge of the lake.

He's not facing me.

"Andy," I yell. He doesn't answer. My heart begins to pound. Why won't he look at me? I call out to him over and over, and every time it goes ignored. Eventually I reach him.

"Why didn't you help me?" I ask. I grip hold of his arm and turn him around, but I can't. Every pull brings the same angle. Why can't I see his face?

I sat up, breathing heavily. Andy lay beside me looking tired and worn. His eyes were closed like he was asleep, but I couldn't help watching his chest for that comforting rise and fall. After what felt like hours, his chest rose up quickly and then deflated.

Something wasn't right. I reached for his hand and squeezed it gently. He didn't move. My heart began to pound as I pushed back the covers and got to my feet. I grabbed my robe and slipped it on, rushing out of the room.

"Seth," I called frantically, knocking on his door. No answer. Grabbing hold of the handle, I turned it and pushed it open. His room was empty, his bed still made and undisturbed. Where was he? Hadn't he come home last night?

"Marta!" I called out, making my way further down the hall. Her bedroom door creaked open and she peered out. One look at my face and she knew something was wrong.

"What is it?" she asked, following me back down to his room.

"I can't rouse him," I said, panicked. My heart thumped in my chest. *Please don't let him die. Not yet.* I stood back as Marta tried to wake him. My hand covered my mouth as I willed myself not to cry.

"He's breathing," Marta sighed with relief. "I'll call the doctor. Can you sit with him?"

I nodded. I walked around and sat on the side of the bed, taking his hand in mine and covering it with my other hand. He was still so damn cold.

I could hear Marta talking in the hallway. I strained to listen, taking in words like *end* and *morphine*. My stomach turned as anxiety began to cripple me. I couldn't stop this. No matter how badly I wanted to freeze time, it kept on moving.

***

Rise and fall. Rise and fall.

My eyes didn't leave his chest as I watched him breathe short, shallow breaths. The doctor had been by and put a drip in to keep him hydrated, and prescribed injections for the pain. He needed such a high dosage that it all but wiped him out. I just sat there watching him sleep, knowing that it wasn't going to be long now.

The last words he had spoken to me had been him trying to convince me to move on—with his best friend, no less. I pulled out my notebook and began to read; anything to distract me from the reality that was happening before me.

New Year's Eve, 2009

"You're telling me that after six hours of fishing, that's all you have?" I stared at the tiny bass, which was bordering on undersized, and laughed.

"In my defense, I did catch a bigger one—only a bird stole it," Seth shot back.

"A bird stole it?" I repeated with a snigger. "That's the best you can come up with?"

"Hey." Andy laughed. I screamed as he stepped forward and hugged me, holding me hostage in his big fishy arms. "You wanna keep making fun of our hunting abilities?" he teased, tickling me as I giggled.

"Let me go," I gasped, tears streaming down my face. "Now I stink as much as you two do."

"Come on, Emsky," Andy growled, kissing my neck. I laughed, struggling to break free from his embrace. "You know you love the way I smell."

I finally broke free and ran into the kitchen, both guys hot on my heels. "So, what's for dinner then? Because that—" I pointed to the lonely little fish, "—just isn't going to do it."

Seth laughed and slapped the fish down on the counter. "Pizza?" He smirked.

I rolled my eyes. "Well, we'd better order, because it will take them ages to deliver. If they even will out here."

It had been Seth's idea to spend New Year's Eve out by the lake. He knew how much I hated holidays. Holidays reminded me of what I'd lost, and how much I still had to lose . . .

My grip on my pen loosened, sending it falling to the floor. Seth featured in my happy memories just as much as Andy did. Why hadn't I noticed that before? I flipped through the pages, memory after memory staring back at me. Seth's role in nearly all of them was pivotal to my happiness. The notebook fell into my lap as I ran my fingers through my hair.

All Seth had ever wanted was my happiness.

He'd watched Andy and me through nine years of love and romance because he could see how happy I was—even if it meant compromising his own emotions. How lucky was I to have two people who would do anything in the world for me?

OUT OF REACH

My stomach churned as I remembered my behavior on the beach earlier in the day. I'd made him feel like shit for not telling me that he was in love with me. What the fuck was that? I knew better than anyone that you couldn't turn off your feelings.

It would've been easier for him to tell me a year ago, or ten years ago. To hide the way he felt in order to preserve our friendship spoke volumes about the kind of man he was.

I had messed things up, and I didn't know how to right them. I didn't know if Seth and I could go back to how we were. I wasn't even sure if I wanted to—because deep down, on some level I wasn't quite ready to admit, I think there was some truth to what Andy had been saying. I think there was a part of me that was in love with Seth. And if there wasn't—I was pretty sure there could be.

Chapter Twenty-Two

Seth

It was after ten in the morning by the time I'd worked up the guts to return to the beach house. I wasn't looking forward to seeing Em or Andy, but it wasn't like I had the time to put it off. One day could mean the difference between being able to make peace or never saying goodbye.

Goodbye.

I dreaded the moment where I'd have to say that. It was so final—but I suppose so was death. I walked in through the back. Marta looked up from the magazine she had in front of her at the table.

"Seth, thank God."

"What's going on?" I asked. Something was wrong. I could feel it. "Is he okay?"

"The doctor's been here. It's not good. He's resting now. He's on a high dose of morphine for the pain, which means he sleeps a lot."

My heart raced as I ran down to his bedroom. Stopping in the doorway, I stared at him lying in the bed, asleep. Em looked up from the armchair. She'd been crying. Her eyes met mine, a fresh wave of tears spilling down her cheeks.

I walked over to her and knelt down. She fell into my arms, sobbing against my chest. I stroked her hair gently with my fingers, my eyes not leaving Andy. He was so pale, his breathing worse than I'd seen it. A breathing tube was in place in his nose, forcing oxygen into his lungs.

"Shh, Em, it's okay," I mumbled.

"I'm not ready to let him go," she whispered, her nails digging into my back. I just held her, knowing there was nothing I could say right then that could make it any easier.

"I'll be back in a second."

Out in the kitchen, I leaned against the counter and sighed. I needed a moment to get myself together so I could be strong for her. I'd spent so much time focused on Em and Andy that I hadn't allowed myself to process what was happening.

Andy was dying. This was it, his last days, and maybe hours. Should I let Deb know that he'd gotten worse? No— the last thing I wanted was for them to be driving upset. I just hoped they would hurry up.

I carried a cup of tea and a chair back into the room.

"Thanks." Em smiled, accepting the cup I held out for her.

I sat the chair next to her and slumped down, snaking my arm around her shoulders.

"Listen." She hesitated, studying the contents of her cup. "I'm sorry for yelling at you yesterday."

I shook my head. "No, look, it's fine. I get it. It must've been a shock." I laughed and shook my head. "I still have no idea why he told you."

"Because she needed to know."

Both Em and I looked over at Andy in surprise. He hadn't moved. His eyes were still closed. I was beginning to think that maybe I'd imagined it, until he spoke again.

"What time is it?"

I laughed and wiped my eyes. Reaching over, I took his hand. "You scared me, man. I thought you'd left me without saying goodbye."

"Yeah? Kind of like the way you stormed out of here yesterday, huh?"

I laughed. "You're a dick. But I love you, Andy."

He managed a smile. "You two need to promise me that you'll look after each other, okay? That's the only thing I want from you: your promises to be there for each other."

"Of course. Don't even worry about that, Andy," I muttered. Em nodded in agreement. "Your mom is on her way," I added.

To my surprise, he laughed. "I knew you'd do that, man. You wouldn't let me go without her saying goodbye. That's why I love you," he said. His voice trailed off as he fell back into a deep sleep. Em sobbed next to me.

"Shh, come here." We stood up. I pulled her toward me, wrapping my arms around her. She couldn't stand the thought of losing him, and the time was getting closer and closer. "I'll be here every step of the way, Em." I reached down and kissed the edge of her jaw, tasting her salty tears.

I looked up and saw Marta standing at the door. She

shifted awkwardly, as if she were embarrassed about interrupting a moment. I smiled, letting her know it was okay.

"There are people here. For the wake."

Shit. I'd forgotten about that. Em turned to me, her eyes wide.

"It's okay. I'll explain to them what's happening." I squeezed her hand as she sat back down. I followed Marta down to the living room.

"Marty." I grinned. Fuck, it had been years since I'd seen him.

He laughed and walked over to greet me. He patted my back as we hugged. "How are ya, Sethie?" He shook his head. "Geez, man, you don't look any different."

I laughed. "Yeah, I wish I could say the same thing about you," I joked. I turned my attention to the blonde standing behind him, cradling a baby. "Are you going to introduce me?"

"Yeah, this is Mandy." He grinned, holding his arm out and motioning for her to come over. She smiled and stepped over to us. "My wife. And this is Bailey, our little boy."

I peered over at the little bundle wrapped in a soft blue-and-white blanket. He made a face and smiled at me, making me laugh.

"He's gorgeous. How old is he?"

"Nearly four weeks. Yeah, we're pretty happy with him," he said, winking at Mandy. She rolled her eyes and nodded. "How's Andy?" he asked, his voice turning serious.

"Not good," I said, wincing. "Unresponsive most of the time now, and in a lot of pain."

"Fuck," he muttered, shaking his head. "This sucks. Poor guy. How's Emily?"

"Barely coping," I replied grimly. "About how you'd expect her to be. His family is on their way." I hesitated. "Look dude, I know you've come a long way . . ."

Marty shook his head. "No, we completely understand. Is there anything we can do? Do you want me to contact the rest of the guys and tell them not to come?"

"I don't even know who's invited."

"He emailed a bunch of us. I'm pretty sure I have most of their numbers. Leave it all to me. You just be there for him. And Emily."

Chapter Twenty-Three

Emily

I didn't leave his side all night. Caught up in my own guilt and sadness, I held his hand in mine, my fingers softly stroking his dry, worn skin. The doctor had just been by to write up some morphine, and Seth was calling his parents.

Andy didn't have much time left.

I watched him as he slipped in and out of consciousness. Every few minutes, he opened up his eyes and stared at me in shock. It was like he didn't even recognize me. Wiping away a stray tear, I took a deep breath. I refused to let myself think of anyone other than Andy. Why hadn't I told him that yes, I was still in love with him? Would it have killed me to lie? He was fucking dying, for Christ's sake.

I wasn't ready to let him go. I needed him, no matter how selfish of me that was. *I needed him.* He was going to die never knowing how much I'd loved him. My feelings for Seth weren't real. We were both grieving for our best friend's impending death. Seth was comforting. He understood. It was easy to confuse that connection for something deeper.

"I'm so angry at you right now," I whispered. "Why did you have to push me away?" His last few weeks on this earth and he'd spent them shoving me into the arms of another man. How was I supposed to accept that? So what if Andy was okay with it? Nobody else was going to be. His parents were the closest thing I had to a family. How would they ever understand my being with Seth?

***

Seth came up behind me. I froze as his fingers grazed my shoulders, his touch incredible against my skin. I needed my mind to stop turning, because all it was doing was confusing me even more.

"His parents are here," he murmured.

I nodded, knowing what I had to do. They deserved to spend some time alone with their son, no matter how hard it would be for me to tear myself away from him.

"Come on, let's get you some fresh air."

I didn't answer as Seth stood me up and walked me out of the room. I passed Andy's mom and dad, unable to meet their eyes. If only they knew what a horrible person I was. What I'd done. What I'd so badly wanted to do.

"Em, I'm worried about you."

We stood on the deck. Seth wrapped his arms around me, his warmth radiating through me. I couldn't move or react; I just stood there, allowing myself to be hugged.

"Talk to me." He tilted my chin up, his eyes meeting mine. I blinked back tears. Where did I even start? How could I put into words what I was feeling?

"I *hate* you for loving me," I whispered.

Hurt filled his expression as he processed my words. He looked shocked and confused. I took a breath and continued, knowing that if I didn't get this out now I never would.

"If you weren't in love with me, then he wouldn't have pushed me away. I hate you for taking that from me. For taking *him* from me."

"Em, you don't mean that. You're upset, and I get it. But

Andy *wants* you to be happy. You don't need to decide anything now, or in a month, or even in a year. This is all about you and when you're ready." He reached forward, his hand cradling my neck as he forced me to look at him.

"I don't want to be happy without him. I don't want to move on."

Chapter Twenty-Four

Seth

It's called the death rattle.

In the final hours before someone dies of a long-term illness, as their body begins to shut down and their lungs begin to fill with fluid, every breath is a struggle, accompanied by a strangling, gurgling sound. Apparently he wasn't in any pain—according to Marta, and confirmed by Google—but it was horrible to witness.

By now, he was unconscious, unresponsive to everyone. He was slowly slipping away. Deb and Karl sat on one side of the bed, Em and I on the other. We hadn't left his side all day. Even in just the last few hours he'd gotten so much worse.

I reached out at took hold of Em's hand. She glanced at me, her green eyes swollen and red from the endless flow of tears. I hadn't cried. I couldn't, because I was sure once I started I wouldn't be able to stop.

"I'm going to make a coffee," I said, getting up. "Can I get you one?" She nodded. "How about you guys?" I asked, looking at Deb and Karl.

"Thanks Seth. A coffee would be nice," Deb sniffed. I touched her on the shoulder as I walked past. She was a wreck—but then again, we all were.

While I waited for the coffee pot to boil, I decided to call Mom. I hadn't spoken to her in a while, though I knew Deb had told her I'd called.

"Seth?" she said, answering on the second ring. Worry filled her voice, and I felt bad. I was the worst son, blocking her out of this. She loved Andy as much as the rest of us did.

"Mom, hey."

"Is he . . . " Her voice broke.

"Not yet. Soon," I said, feeling sick. I leaned over the counter and stared at the black marble top. "He's pretty close to the end now. Deb and Karl are here."

"Good," she said, relieved. "I'm glad they got there in time. How's Em?"

"Not great," I sighed. "She's coping, but barely. I'm worried about her, Mom."

"I know you are, honey. You just need to be there for her. There's not much else you can do." She was right, but it didn't make me feel any better.

"I better go," I said with a sigh. "I'll call you later. Love you," I said, rubbing the bridge of my nose.

"Love you, too."

***

I carried the coffees, two in each hand, back to the bedroom.

"Thanks," mumbled Karl, taking both his and Deb's. Em didn't respond as I placed hers next to her. "The priest is on his way now."

I nodded. Andy wasn't religious, but I knew this was more for them than him.

I sat down, cradling my drink in my hands. My mind was filled with regrets. Why hadn't I spent more time with him over the past few months? Fuck work—I should've quit and hung out with him. I felt like I'd missed out on so much. It wasn't fair. He was only twenty-six.

Fucking cancer. I laughed, thinking about the tattoo on his back. Would his parents ever see it? Both Deb and Em looked me with puzzled expressions.

"I just remembered . . . his back," I finished, my voice low. Realization dawned on Em's face and she snorted. "I'm sorry," I said to Deb, still chuckling.

Then I had an idea. I jumped up and walked over the wardrobe where his video recorder sat. I picked it up and handed it to Deb.

"He was never without this damn thing the last few weeks."

She smiled and opened the viewing screen. Fresh tears filled her eyes as she pressed play. I sat back down, placing my arm around Em as she snuggled against me. Andy's voice filled the room and my heart jumped.

We listened in silence as Deb lived through Andy's final days. Her hand flew to her mouth as muffled sobs escaped from her. I closed my eyes, listening, replaying the events in my head as I heard them.

"He made you do all this?" Deb gasped. That was after

the bull riding.

I laughed and nodded.

"That's Andy," she smiled. "What the hell?" she cried.

I swallowed a laugh as Andy's voice explained *"Cancer fucked me over, so I'm fucking it over right back."* I glanced over at Em, who was staring at the small tattoo on her wrist, a shadow of a smile on her face.

At 1:33a.m., Andy took his last breath.

I thought I was ready, but nothing really prepares you for that moment. He was there, and then he wasn't. I saw his chest rise and fall for the last time, and then he was gone. I felt...empty. It was like a part of me had died right along with him.

Em began to sob loudly next to me. I stood up and wrapped my arms around her, holding her close to me as her body shook, determined to protect her from the world of hurt she was feeling. Deb and Karl sobbed quietly, embracing each other.

He's gone. I can't believe he's gone.

My heart pounded as I held Em, the finality of the moment beginning to sink in. My best friend was gone. I'd never be able to talk to him, to hear his voice, or joke with him again. She jumped up suddenly.

"Seth." Deb motioned for me to leave with her and Karl. I glanced at Em, who was now kneeling beside his bed, clutching his hand. "She needs a few minutes alone with him. She'll be okay."

Will she? I wasn't so sure.

Chapter Twenty-Five

Emily

I held his hand, my tears falling uncontrollably. He was gone. No matter how much I'd tried to prepare for this moment, clutching his lifeless hand between mine was unbearable.

I can't believe you left me. Why didn't you fight harder?

I climbed into bed beside him, desperate to feel his body up against mine one more time. The warmth was beginning to fade, just like my will to live. I didn't want a life without him in it. This wasn't fair.

I lay in his arms, crying.

Please come back. I'll do anything for you not to leave

me.

I racked my mind for a memory, anything to cling onto while lying there next to him. Anything that I could use to convince myself I hadn't lost him. But it was hopeless. My head was a mess. I'd lost the one person I thought would be there for me forever. The one person who I knew loved me, no matter what. My heart was heavy. I could have died right there alongside him and it wouldn't have mattered.

None of it mattered anymore. Nothing.

Chapter Twenty-Six

Emily

A week had passed. It had been a whole week since he'd left me. I never thought time could pass so slowly and so fast at the same time. I was a mess. I felt like I was moving in slow motion. Nothing made sense to me anymore.

It was the day of his funeral. I hadn't slept. I'd barely slept at all since he'd gone. Sleeping meant remembering and I wasn't ready to do that yet. We had left the beach house and come home the day after he passed. Deb had insisted I stay with them, and I was thankful that I didn't have to be alone.

I sat at my dressing table, waiting. It was barely nine in the morning, yet I sat there in my black dress, ready.

Waiting to say my final goodbye to the man that had been my family for the last fourteen years.

I'd dressed for him today—in his favorite dress, wearing his favorite perfume with my hair pinned to the side, just how he loved it. I didn't bother with makeup. For one, I hadn't stopped crying for long enough to be able to apply it, and second, Andy had always told me how beautiful I was without it.

For all the pain I felt right then, I wouldn't take anything back. I wouldn't change anything. All the pain in the world was worth one day of knowing Andy.

Focus on the good.

I pulled out my notebook and flicked open a page. I began to read.

Christmas morning. 2002.

The first Christmas without my parents.

It had been less than a month since the accident. I couldn't imagine ever not feeling the way I did that morning as I rose to an empty house. No tree, no presents and no reason to acknowledge the day. Even though Andy's family had taken me in, I was back here, the night before Christmas, alone with my emotions. I didn't want to celebrate with anyone else. I just wanted my parents back.

It was my fault they'd been killed. Every time I closed my eyes, my own words screamed back at me. I wish I'd been born to someone else.

"Em?"

I looked up and into Seth's eyes. He walked over and cradled me in his arms while Andy knelt down in front of me.

"What are you doing here? We've been so worried," *Andy said. He took my hands in his. "Have you been here all night?"*

I nodded. "The settlement is tomorrow. I just needed one last day to..." My voice trailed off. I couldn't even say it. "Besides, I don't want to celebrate Christmas. It's just another day like every other day." Except more than any other day, today I was reminded of how little I'd appreciated what I'd had until I'd lost it.

"Okay," Andy said, as if it were that simple. "Then we're not celebrating it either."

"What? You have to," I protested.

"Nope," Seth chimed in. "We're with you, Em. We are not going to leave you, especially not today."

I closed the book and smiled as I pushed it back into my pocket. That Christmas had been spent sitting in my empty living room eating pizza and drinking soda. They had given up their Christmas because I hadn't been ready to move on. They were always there for me. Every moment, the two of them were by my side.

"Em?"

I looked up and saw Seth standing in my doorway.

"How did you get in?" I asked. I hadn't even heard him knock, and I was pretty sure Deb and Karl had left ages ago.

"Spare key," he smiled. He walked over and sat down on the bed next to me. "Are you okay?" he asked. His hand found its way to mine, his fingers entwining themselves with mine.

"Not really," I said with a laugh. I was burying my boyfriend today. How was I supposed to be okay with that?

"Silly question, huh?"

"A little," I agreed. Sighing, I stood up and threw myself back on the bed. I stared at the ceiling, feeling sick. "I don't want to say goodbye to him." He lay back with me. I rested my head on his shoulder. "I keep thinking it's not real, you know? That I'm just having an awful nightmare and I'll wake up and everything will be normal."

"I feel that too," Seth admitted. "I keep hearing his voice. Every time I close my eyes I see his face." He hesitated. "We have to go."

I swallowed, nodding my head. I knew we had to leave.

Seth sat up and reached for my jacket, carefully arranging it over my shoulders. "It's cold out," he said, his voice gruff.

***

Everyone was staring at me. I could feel their eyes on me as I sat down in the front row of the church—eyes full of pity and sadness. They felt sorry for me. I was the girl who had lost both parents tragically, and now I was burying my boyfriend. Only I didn't want their pity.

All I wanted was Andy.

My gaze locked on the white coffin that lay in front of me. An array of lilacs and white roses had expertly been arranged on top, and a framed photo of Andy sat in the center. I studied the picture. It was from a year ago, before the cancer had come back. He looked happy.

I felt Seth's hand close over my own. I glanced up at him. He smiled, his eyes empty. I hadn't noticed the dark circles around them before. He looked about how I felt. Taking a deep breath, I closed my eyes, imagining that it was Andy sitting next to me, supporting me.

I don't remember much of the service. I remember standing up in front, staring at the white and brass coffin that lay in front of me, my heart broken. All I could think about was him, lying inside that wooden box. I'd never see him again. I'd never feel his touch against me. I'd never kiss those lips again. I trailed my finger along the edge of coffin as tears rolled down my cheeks. Seth stood next to me, his eyes red and swollen. His hand never left mine.

People stood up to talk about what a brave, wonderful man he had been. There were so many people crammed into that tiny church that it was ridiculous. I wanted to laugh. Most of these people I'd never even met. How could they stand there and mourn him when they'd obviously not cared enough to see him during his illness?

I felt Seth shift in his seat next to me. He was the only one who understood. Regardless of what had happened in the last few days, Seth was the only thing keeping me going right then. Everything else felt numb…dead. How did trivial shit like living and breathing matter anymore? Simple: it didn't.

"Are you okay for a minute?" Seth mumbled to me.

I nodded, confused. What was he doing? I watched him as he stood up and straightened his suit jacket. He walked over to the edge of the stage and whispered something to the minister, who nodded.

He's going to speak.

He cleared his throat and adjusted the microphone. "I wasn't planning on speaking. I don't have anything prepared, but I wanted to say something."

He lifted his head and stared at me, as if I were the only person in the church. I smiled and nodded, wiping away what felt like a never-ending stream of tears. The church was so quiet you could hear the sound of his breathing through the speakers. Taking a breath, he continued.

"I thought I was prepared to lose my best friend. His death wasn't sudden. It wasn't unexpected. I'd had plenty of time to ready myself for what I knew was eventually going to happen. But you can never really prepare yourself to lose someone. No matter how much warning you have, or how often you tell yourself they're in a better place now, it still sucks and it still hurts." My heart jumped as his voice broke. His gaze fell to the floor before he took another deep breath and continued. "I was lucky to have eighteen years with Andy. I try and tell myself that I was lucky to have known him at all, but I'm selfish. I wanted more. He was the kind of guy who put everyone else before himself. His biggest worry was being forgotten, but as anyone who really knew him would know, he was unforgettable."

He raised his head and looked me in the eyes as I struggled to control my sobbing.

"Andy, you were one in a million. I loved you like a brother and I'm forever grateful of all the wonderful memories you've left me with."

A loud cry escaped from me as he walked over and touched the coffin.

"I love you, man," he whispered.

He walked back over to me. I stood up, wrapping my arms around him as *I Will Remember You* by Sarah McLachlan began to drift through the speakers. Until then, I'd been barely holding it together. But as the lyrics floated around me, I lost it completely. I began to bawl. Seth closed the small gap between us, wrapping his arms even tighter around me. *This isn't happening.* Any moment I was going to wake up, and it would all be over. Life couldn't be this cruel.

Only it *was* happening. And there was nothing I could do to change that.

***

After the service, we sat in the kitchen at his parents' house. I was sick of smiling. I was sick of pretending to every person that approached me that I was okay.

Because I wasn't. And I wouldn't ever be again.

Seth sat next to me. He held my hand under the table, every now and then squeezing it just to let me know he was there for me. There were people everywhere, but I had never felt more alone. With the exception of Seth, none of these people understood. I hated thinking it, but not even Deb could understand this.

"Do you need to get some air?" Seth asked. I nodded. He stood up, and I moved with him. I followed wordlessly as he led me outside, down the back toward the huge oak tree. We sat down, me snuggled into the crest of his arm.

"We used to climb this tree all the time. See who could

go higher. Deb used to come out and yell at us." He glanced up and smiled. "See that branch?" I nodded. "When he was nine, he fell off that branch and broke his arm."

I smiled, finding the sound of Seth's chuckling soothing.

"I remember spending every weekend down at the skate park with you two, because Andy had insisted if I wanted to be in your group then I had to," I smiled, wiping away tears.

Seth sighed, his fingers stroking my hand.

"I miss him too, Em. The pain is never going to go away, but we just have to try and get through it. We have to do it for him."

Chapter Twenty-Seven

Emily

It had been two weeks since Andy's death. Every day that passed was supposed to be easier. It wasn't. I missed him so much, and I missed Seth, but the guilt I felt when I thought about Seth…it was too much.

My phone vibrated. I picked it up and saw another message from Seth—the tenth today, and it was only two in the afternoon. A wave of irritation rushed through me. Didn't he get that I didn't want to see him right now? I didn't want to see anyone.

You don't want to see me, and that's fine, but I need to know you're okay.

"I'll be okay when you leave me alone," I muttered,

tossing the phone across the bed. I rolled over and pulled the covers up over me. Yeah, I was in bed. So what? So what if I'd spent a good part of the last two weeks in bed?

I snuggled up against his pillow. It still smelled like him. If I closed my eyes and imagined hard enough, it was almost like he was there with me. But he wasn't. He was dead, and I was alone.

***

My eyes opened. It took me a moment to adjust to the darkness that surrounded me. Cold, I felt over my stomach and realized the covers had slipped off me. I moved over in the bed, over to his side, rearranging the blankets over me.

The clock stared back at me. 3:04.

Another day gone.

Something hard dug into my side. I reached underneath me and pulled out my phone. More messages, more missed calls—although this time from Seth and Deb.

Deb came around every day. She would bring food— which would usually end up in the trash—and sit with me. She didn't try to make me talk, or get up, because she understood. Everything I was going through, she was going through too. Just having each other was a comfort on some level.

I pushed back the covers and stood up, the urge to pee too strong to ignore.

I should really shower. But I couldn't. I couldn't do anything. It was like I was stuck, frozen in this stage and I couldn't move past it. I wasn't eating, I didn't get dressed. All I did was sleep.

Because in my dreams, he's still with me.

Chapter Twenty-Eight

Seth

I sat at my desk, staring at my laptop. I thought coming back to work would help me keep my mind of things. And for the most part, it did. Until something reminded me of Andy. And then I'd lose it. He'd been gone for three weeks and five days, and it had been almost as long since I'd seen Em. I hated how much my heart ached at the thought of her. Losing Andy had been hard enough; losing Em too was unbearable.

The soft rapping on my office door caught my attention. I looked up. My boss, Ian, smiled at me sympathetically. They had been surprisingly supportive of everything—

much more so than I had expected.

"Are you sure you want to be here, Seth? I told you to take as much time as you needed."

"Thanks, but I think I need the distraction, you know?"

Ian nodded. "If there's anything we can do, let us know." He smiled again before walking off.

Sighing, I reached for my phone, checking for a message that I knew wouldn't be there. How was Em doing? She wouldn't answer my texts or calls, but that didn't stop me from trying. I got little bits of information from Deb, but even she was struggling to get through to her. I was so worried, but I had no idea what else to do.

After lunch, I walked back into my office and found a package on my desk. I picked up the package. My heart began to pound as I saw the handwriting. I didn't need to check the return address to know it was from Andy.

I sat down, the package in front of me. When had he sent this? And why had it taken so long to reach me? It had been nearly four weeks since he'd died. I ran my fingers over the smooth wrapping, staring at his handwriting. It was heavier than a letter, but not much thicker.

What was it?

I swallowed. Maybe this was my way back into her life. A gift from Andy…she would have to see me for this. There was no way she couldn't.

I picked up the phone and dialed Ian's extension.

"Yes, Seth?"

"If it's okay, I might take some time," I said, hesitating.

"Of course it is. Just keep in touch, okay?"

***

I stood at her door, turning the package over in my hands. What if she still refused to see me? She wasn't doing well, I knew that from Deb. I was so worried about her, and I felt so helpless. Taking a deep breath, I rapped on the door.

Nobody answered. I glanced around. I couldn't imagine she would've gone anywhere. Deb said she wasn't even getting out of bed. I knocked again. Still no answer. I lifted my arm and felt above the door frame for the spare key I knew Andy had left there. I sighed, relieved, as my fingers grasped the cold metal.

I walked inside. The apartment was quiet—quiet enough for me to wonder if she was even home, but from what Deb had told me, she hadn't been leaving the house. I crept down the hallway to her room. My heart sank when I saw her—lying in bed, asleep, her hair tangled and her face so pale.

I didn't want to wake her on the off chance that she hadn't been sleeping. I walked back out and sat down on the sofa, crossing my leg over my knee with the package in front of me.

No matter how ordinary she'd looked, just the sight of her had my heart racing. I'd wait all day for her if I had to.

Chapter Twenty-Nine

Emily

I jumped as I walked into the living room and saw Seth sitting there. Instinctively, I tightened my robe as he looked up, his eyes meeting mine. It hurt so much seeing him, because seeing him made me remember. And I couldn't. It hurt too much.

"What are you doing here?" I asked, clearing my throat.

He picked up a neatly wrapped package that sat on the coffee table in front of him.

"I wanted to give you this. It arrived at work today." He paused, glancing back up at me. "It's from Andy."

My eyes widened. I sank onto the sofa, feeling as though

I'd been hit in the stomach. Seth held the package out to me. I took it, examining the writing on the front. His writing. My name.

With shaking hands I unwrapped the package, careful not to damage the scrawl of writing. Two things fell into my lap: a small pink box and a letter with 'Read me first' scrawled across the front. Tears rolled down my cheeks as I opened the letter.

Emsky,

Firstly, stop crying. I know you well enough to know that's exactly what you'd be doing right now. Smile because we got to spend some amazing years together, don't cry for what we missed out on.

From the moment I saw you, I knew you were the girl for me. Everything about you exuded confidence and excitement. I lost count of the number of times I fell asleep with your name on my lips, your smile in my memory.

The day you became mine was the best day of my life. I couldn't believe that I had managed to snare you. I felt like I'd somehow fooled you into loving me, and that at any

minute you'd realize how much better you could do than
me. But you didn't. For whatever insane reason, you were
as into me as I was you.

Now I want you to open the box.

I set the letter down in my lap and reached for the box,
wiping the tears from my eyes. A delicate white ribbon tied
into a perfect bow sat on top of the glossy, light pink
colored top. Taking hold of an end, I pulled until it
unraveled and floated from my hands to the floor.

My hands shook as I lifted the lid. Inside sat a bracelet.
Looped onto the fine silver band were a series of beautiful
pink and silver charms. I examined each one, rolling them
gently between my forefinger and thumb.

"Oh God," I whispered, sobbing. The bracelet was the
most precious thing I'd ever seen—even more so because it
was from Andy. Holding it, I felt close to him. *He would've*
been the last person to touch these delicate little charms.

With the bracelet firmly grasped in my palm, I picked up
the letter.

I hate the thought of us missing out on so much. There are so many things I wanted to experience with you. This is my way of playing a small part of that. Each charm represents a milestone in your life—things I so badly wish I could be there to experience with you: your wedding day, the birth of your first child.

In a small way, now I'll be right there with you through each of these things. Please don't be sad, Em. Think of all the wonderful times we had, and all the amazing things you still have to look forward to in your life. Most of all, let your heart love again. If that is the only thing you do for me, then I will have died happy.

You deserve everything in the world, Emsky. You cared for me every second of my illness. I never once felt alone, or afraid, with you by my side. You put me first, just as you have since the beginning. Now it's time to put Emily first.

Love you forever,

Andy xx

I handed the letter to Seth and curled up on the sofa, the bracelet still balled up in my fist, my arms hugging my stomach. I missed him so much. Why did he have to write me that? I couldn't do this without him.

"Em…" Seth knelt beside me. He pushed the hair from my face, his blue eyes filled with concern. "It's okay, Em." He put his arms around me and whispered in my ear over and over. But it wasn't. It would never be okay.

"It's not okay," I cried, pushing him away. "He's gone and I can't love you, no matter how much I want to. I just can't! Everything about you makes me think of him," I sobbed.

His hands gripped my wrists firmly as he fought me. Loving Seth meant forgetting Andy. Guilt tore through me as I began to hyperventilate.

"Calm down, Em," he ordered, his voice thick with emotion. He held me to his chest. "Breathe. Forget about everything and just focus on breathing. Everything will be okay."

How could he be so calm? How was he always so in control? I so badly wanted to be with him, but it couldn't…I just couldn't…

"Do you love me, Em?"

"It doesn't matter!" I jerked away from him. Why didn't he get it? "We can never happen. The memory of him will always be there, lurking in the background, as a reminder of how selfish and greedy I am."

"Selfish?" he laughed. "You devoted your life to caring for him, Em. How is that selfish?"

I breathed in sharply as his fingers pushed my hair from my eyes. "You didn't answer my question."

"You didn't ask one," I muttered.

"Do you love me?" he whispered.

"How can you ask me that after we just buried him?" I cried.

"Because it's what he would want me to do, Em. He loved—loves you more than anything. Knowing you're going to be okay is the only thing that mattered to him. Your happiness was all he ever cared about. Even when he realized he couldn't make you happy anymore."

"How can I ever be happy again?" I whispered.

He pulled me into his arms as I cried, stroking my hair.

Chapter Thirty

Emily

Seth glanced my way and squeezed my hand. I smiled at him. We were on our way back to the beach house. It was the place I felt closest to Andy, and right then that was what I needed. Once again, Seth had dropped everything for me. I felt like I was the only thing that mattered in his eyes, and that was something I could never repay him for.

Having Seth back in my life didn't make dealing with the loss of Andy any easier, but having someone by my side, that felt my pain, did help. In his own way, I could see Seth was suffering too. It was so easy to trap myself away in my little bubble, believing that nobody else was as affected as I was. But that wasn't true: Andy's death had hurt lots of people, and people dealt with things differently.

With my head leaning against the window, I began reading. Every day I read through each page, some days two or three times. I was so desperate to feel closer to him and I felt like my memories—and now my bracelet—were the only ways I could do that.

October 2005. First sexual experience.

I crawled onto Andy's bed carefully, not wanting to hurt him. He chuckled and shook his head, his dark eyes sparkling at me.

"I'm not going to break, Em," he said.

"I know. I just don't want to hurt you." I kneeled over him, one leg on either side of his waist. He grinned, his hands running up over my thighs.

"I think this needs to go," he said, tugging at the oversized T-shirt—his shirt—which ran down to my mid-thigh.

"I thought you liked this on me," I pouted playfully, my fingers lifting up the hem.

"I like it better off you," he murmured, eyeing my bare thighs.

Straightening myself up, I gripped the hem of the shirt

and lifted it over my head, a shiver racing down my back as his fingers trailed upward to my breasts. I was naked, completely exposed, and totally his.

"Fuck, you're beautiful," he murmured softly. "Are you sure you're ready?"

"I'm ready," I promised. I shifted slowly in his lap, grinding myself against his erection. He moaned, growing even harder beneath me. He reached down and, lifting his hips, shuffled out of his boxer shorts, his hardness pressing against my pussy.

He retrieved a condom from the side table and broke it open. I watched him as he rolled it on.

"What?" he asked, amused.

"Nothing, I've just . . ." I wasn't going to admit it was my first time. We might have been best friends, but that was one thing we didn't discuss. I felt so silly, but other than during a curious late-night internet search, I hadn't even seen a penis before.

"Are you okay?" he asked. Great, now he was worried about me. I nodded, and then randomly began to laugh, which made him look even more concerned.

"I'm fine," I said, forcing myself to calm down. "It's

just, this is my first time." I closed my eyes and waited for his laughter to ring in my ears. Instead, I felt his hands roll over my hips, his touch sending my senses into overdrive.

"Why are you embarrassed about that?" he said with a grin. "I think it's cute."

"I don't want you to think I'm cute," I grumbled. "I want you to think I'm sexy, and confident, and beautiful."

He propped himself up on his elbows, his lips pressing against mine in a deep, slow kiss. My nipples hardened as they brushed past his bare chest. I exhaled sharply as he stroked the curve of my back, his fingers magical against my skin.

"You are all those things, Em. You have no idea what you do to me," he whispered.

It had been just three days after his diagnosis, and fifteen days since we'd officially begun dating. We didn't know what the road ahead held. The prognosis could've been worse, but the chemotherapy and radiation were likely to make him really sick.

I'd wanted him to know I was there for him in every way. I'd wanted to give myself to him completely. It had been awkward and funny—nothing like I'd imagined it would be—but it had also been perfect, because I loved him.

"Do you want anything?"

I looked up, surprised that we were stopped at a gas station and I hadn't even realized. Shutting the notebook, I pushed it back into my pocket.

"No, I'm good. Thanks," I said, smiling.

"You look a little happier," he observed, raising his eyebrows. His blue eyes studied me. "It's good to see you smile again."

It felt good to smile. There hadn't been too many times over the last few weeks where I could think about Andy without bursting into tears.

Seth got out and walked around to the side of the car. I fiddled with my bracelet, rolling one of the tiny charms between my fingers. It was such an Andy thing in so many ways—romantic and thoughtful. And it had made me realize that I had so many things to look forward to. I'd been lucky enough to share so much with Andy. Maybe one day I'd be ready to create some new memories.

***

"Em." Seth's voice cut through my dreams. I stirred, opening my eyes. We were there. "Are you ready?" he asked.

I nodded. We stepped out of the car. I walked toward the front door while Seth got our things. My heart pounded as I neared the door, my feet heavy as I forced one foot in front of the other. The night of his death was playing over and over in my head. Here, I couldn't escape the memories; I had to face them.

It had been Seth's idea to come back. He thought it would help me, to get back to where his last moments had been spent. And maybe it would. Along with our bags, Seth had a box. It contained a few of Andy's things: the videos of our trip, some old photos of the three of us together . . . and his list.

We were there to finish the final few things off his bucket list. Neither of us had looked at it yet. We'd decided it was something that needed to be done there, where all three of us had been together. After what Andy had made us do while he was still alive, I was more than a little bit nervous to see what else he had on that list.

I walked inside, my skin tingling. It was freezing. The curtains were drawn, and the darkness of the day was making me feel depressed. I flipped on one of the lights, even though it was only five in the afternoon. The light filled the room, instantly making it feel warmer and homier. The place looked just as we'd left it—only cleaner.

Seth walked in behind me. He dropped our bags and put his hands around the front of my shoulders, hugging me against him. I reached up, my hand closing over his. I was so lucky to have him.

"I insist on covering some of the cost, staying here again," I said.

"No, it's all sorted. The agent managed to work out a really good deal with the owner, anyway. Besides, it's only money."

I nodded and walked around into the living room. Sitting down on the sofa, I set the box down on the coffee table and stared at it. So many memories waited for me inside, and as happy as they were, reliving them was painful. Seth sat next to me. He handed me a soda.

"Thanks."

"Are you ready for this, Em? Because we can do it later. Take as much time as you need."

"I'm ready," I said, my voice thick with emotion. Was I

ready? No, but I wasn't sure I'd ever be. My hands shook as they lifted the lid off the box. I pulled out the folded-up list, and the handful of photos that lay in the bottom under the weight of the videotapes and his camera. I flipped through photo after photo of the three of us, together. Smiling. *Happy.*

Taking a deep breath, I unfolded the list. My heart pounded as I laid it down in front of me so we could both read it.

Andy's bucket list

 # Cliff jumping

 # Get a tattoo

 # Ride a bull

 # NASCAR

 # Dinner in a Michelin-star restaurant

 # Camping in the backyard

 # Learn another language

 # Swim with the sharks

 # Spend the night in a jumping castle on the lake

 # Hot-air ballooning over the ocean

 # Get drunk and make prank calls

 # Help Em and Seth move on

Wow. There were things on there that he'd done ages ago. He had been working on this list for months. Things began to make sense: his sudden desire to learn French, his insisting we go to Decant—one of the top restaurants in the state—even though he could barely eat. He had been slowly working his way through this list and I'd never known it. Tears began to form as my eyes fell on the final item on the list.

 # Tell Em that I love her every single day

I reached up and wiped away the tears. Seth's arm crept behind my back as he held me close, letting me know he was there for me. I reached into my bag and pulled out my pen, drawing a line through the words.

"Because he did that. Every single day he told me he loved me, right up to the day he died." I began to sob. Seth's fingers stroked my hairline as all the stress and anxiety I had built up over the past few weeks began to tumble out.

This was all so wrong. Andy hadn't deserved to die.

How could such an amazing, wonderful, loving person's life be over so soon? It didn't make any sense. Nothing in this stupid world made any sense any more. I hated life. I hated living. And more than anything, I hated death.

"Shh, it's okay. He loved you more than anything else in this world." Seth held me in the warmth of his arms, my head resting against his chest. He held me as I cried. I traced my fingers over the scrawl of Andy's writing, as if touching the dried ink would somehow bring me closer to him. I missed him so much, but I had to be strong for him. As much as I wanted to hide in bed and wait for death to take me too, Andy had wanted me to get on with my life. As impossible as that felt at that moment, I had to try.

"Let's do this. Let's go out and do these things for him," I mumbled.

Chapter Thirty-One

Seth

I had no idea how hard it would be to book a hot-air balloon ride on such short notice. Three hundred dollars and a lot of groveling later, and I'd finally managed to convince a company to squeeze us in by giving the guy a sob story about living out my best friend's final wishes.

It was just after five in the morning when I woke Em. Tangled in my embrace, she hadn't left my arms all night. I had barely slept because I'd been too consumed with watching her sleep. There was something beautiful about the way she looked sleeping in my arms, with all her walls down. I could see the real her, vulnerabilities and all.

I tickled the tip of her nose, chuckling as she screwed it up, smacking at my fingers with her hand.

Her eyes opened and narrowed in on mine. "Have you been watching me sleep again? Creepy, Seth."

I laughed. If only she knew. Still dressed in yesterday's clothes, I dug a fresh change out of my suitcase and walked toward the main bathroom, leaving the one in the bedroom for her to use.

"We'll have to be gone in twenty minutes," I called out. I took her muffled reply as an okay.

I turned the on the coffee pot on my way past, the aroma of fresh coffee beans soaking into the air. Grabbing a towel from the cupboard, I showered, dressed, and had the coffee ready all before Em had even appeared.

"Here," I smirked, sliding a mug across the counter. "You look like you could use it."

She grunted at me. "How are you so functional this early? There's something wrong with you," she added, her eyes twinkling at me.

"There's plenty wrong with me, but enjoying mornings isn't one of them," I retorted. "Mornings make you feel alive." Her face fell, and I felt bad. "Sorry," I muttered, cursing myself. *Mornings make you feel alive? Am I stupid?*

"It's fine," she said, a small smile on her lips. "I manage to work every conversation, every word, back to Andy anyway."

I sighed, the pain I felt for her rising inside me. "It will get easier, Em."

Because I was such an expert on losing the people I loved.

***

Daylight hadn't broken yet. I suppose if it had, it would've defeated the purpose of a sunrise balloon ride. Conveniently, the meeting point for the takeoff was only a couple of miles from the beach house.

Em shivered next to me as we walked across the sand and over to the grassy dune where the balloon was sitting. It was the first time I'd seen one of those things up close, and it was fucking huge.

"It's, um, big." Em swallowed, her eyes wide as she stared up at the silver and orange balloon. I chuckled and put my arm around her back. I was shocked when she'd managed the cliff jump with her fear of heights; this was going to be terrifying for her.

"You can wait here if you're scared," I teased. Her body stiffened as she glowered at me, her eyebrows rising. I laughed. She was so damn easy to wind up.

We approached the guy who appeared to be in charge—because anyone holding a clipboard had to have some sort of authority.

He smiled at us and extended his arm. "Seth and Emily?" he asked, shaking my hand.

I nodded. "That's us. Thanks so much for squeezing us in."

"Happy to have you here. We'll be taking off in about five minutes. It's a perfect day, so just enjoy it." He winked at us and then walked over to one of the other couples, leaving us alone.

"Scared?" I asked Em, nudging her shoulder. "I mean, it doesn't look all that secure, considering how far from the ground we're gonna be."

"Oh shut up," she grumbled. "Are you purposely trying to scare me?"

I laughed. "I didn't think it was possible to scare you."

"Yeah," she said, her tone falling serious. She glanced

out over the water. "It used to be like that. Now, not so much."

Stepping through the gate and into the balloon, I held Em's hand. She was looking a little green, and we hadn't even left the ground yet. I laughed and kissed her head. She was so cute when she was nervous, especially when she tried to hide it.

"Here," I said, putting my arm around her shoulders as she nestled into me. Being so close to her felt so natural, even with her knowing how I felt about her . . . and wondering if she felt the same way.

We hadn't really spoken about what was said that day since . . . well, since that day. It had kind of been swept under the rug with all that had happened with Andy dying.

She squealed into my chest, laughing as the balloon began to rise.

"You're missing the best part," I said, smiling into her hair as I held her. She clung to me for dear life as we rose higher and higher, refusing to turn around and see the amazing view.

"Come on. I refuse to let you miss this," I said.

She groaned, but slowly turned around, her grip on me tightening with every step. Her eyes widened. "Wow," she murmured. "That's beautiful."

"Andy would be proud of you," I said as she gazed out over the dark sky where the red glow of the sun had begun to break through.

"Proud of me how?" she scoffed.

"For facing your fears. For getting out there and doing this for him. Don't underestimate how strong you are, Em. You might not feel it, but you're one of the strongest people I know."

She smiled, resting her head on my shoulder. She sighed as she gazed out over the stunning view. The sky was a beautiful mix of reds and oranges. It was spectacular.

"I can't figure out why this was on his list," Em mumbled.

"I imagine that it was probably something he wanted to do with you." I studied her face as she stared up at the stars. Her creamy porcelain skin glowed in the soft light of the full moon. Her lips parted into a smile as she turned to me.

"Do you think he's up there, watching?" she asked.

"Definitely," I smirked. "Andy wouldn't miss this. I

think he's always watching over you." She nodded, as if she was happy with that thought.

We floated around for the next half an hour, drinking champagne and snacking on fresh strawberries. *I could spend every morning this way.* It was amazing what these experiences were doing to push us out of our comfort zones. Every task brought with it the realization that life is short, and we needed to push ourselves to get the most out of it. What was the point in sitting at home wishing things were different?

Even in death, Andy was pushing us to face our fears.

***

"So what now?" Em asked, smiling at me.

After the balloon ride, we had driven out to Vicker's Point and gone hiking, and had lunch down by the creek. Then we had gone into town and done some shopping. Now, it was just after six in the evening and we were driving back to the beach house. I was beat, but there was more planned. It was time to cross another thing off Andy's list.

"Now we go back to the beach house. Everything should

be ready," I added, wiggling my eyebrows.

"What have you planned?" she asked, narrowing her eyes.

"You'll see."

We left the shopping in the car and I led her down the beach. She laughed as soon as we walked over the hill and she saw the surprise. It wasn't much of a surprise, because it was kind of hard to hide the inflatable jumping castle that was floating on the water.

"My God." She giggled, her hand covering her mouth. "I wondered what that big blob was from the sky! How the hell did you pull that off?"

"I have connections." I grinned. "Come on. Dinner will be getting cold."

"Dinner?" she repeated. Her face was glowing. It felt so good to see her smile. I'd been surprised at how easy it had been to find a company willing to bring a castle all the way out there and set it up on the water for the night. I was paying extra for the private chef who was preparing us a three-course meal, but it was worth it to see her happy.

We walked to the edge of the water and over the inflatable ramp into the bright yellow and blue castle. Em laughed as it swayed beneath us, each step like walking through a vat full of marshmallow. Losing her balance, she crashed into me, sending us both into a fit of giggles.

"Good thing I don't get seasick," she joked. She sat down next to the tabletop that had been placed in the center of the castle.

"Good thing for me, you mean. I can just imagine you throwing up all over the place."

She reached over and shoved my arm.

"Anyway, I hope you're hungry."

Em looked up as a formally dressed waiter stepped onto the castle, juggling two perfectly plated appetizers.

"Salmon ravioli." The waiter smiled, setting the appetizers down in front of us. The smell of butter, cream, and salmon wafted around me. My stomach rumbled loudly as my mouth watered.

"Wow, this looks amazing," Em said. She picked up her fork and eased it under one of the delicate pillows of pasta, scooping it into her mouth. She closed her eyes and smiled. "So good."

She was right: it was delicious. As were the confit duck legs we had for main, and the rich double-chocolate mousse that was served for dessert.

"That was quite possibly the best meal I've ever had." She sighed and lay back on the blanket I'd spread out where the tabletop—which had been removed by the waiter—had been. Throwing a couple more blankets over the top of her, I crawled into our makeshift bed, resting my head on my elbow.

"I can't figure out why this was on his list." Em laughed.

I studied her face as she stared up at the stars. Her creamy smooth skin glowed in the soft light of the full moon. Her lips parted into a smile as she turned to me. "Do you really think he's up there, watching?" It was the second time she'd asked me that today.

"I think he's always with you, Em."

Chapter Thirty-Two

Emily

We spent the whole week at the beach house before we went back home. Trying to get back into a normal routine without Andy was hard. Because life without Andy wasn't normal—it was different, and scary, and lonely.

It had been eleven weeks since Andy had died, and every day I thanked God for Seth. Without him, I don't know how I would have coped with the past few weeks. He was always there, always making sure I was okay.

***

My phone beeped. I picked it up, knowing it would be Seth. He always texted after work, just to check in on me. I smiled as his name flashed up.

I just saw a guy walking down the street in a Batman costume. That was the highlight of my day. How was yours?

I giggled and replied.

My day was good. Work, and more work. About to watch Game of Thrones if you want to come over? Bring some dinner and I might let you in.

A goofy grin spread across my lips as I pressed send. It shocked me how much I looked forward to seeing him. Even his messages made my heart race a little faster. How much of that was me trying to fill the gap that Andy had left, and how much of that was my feelings for Seth intensifying? I struggled to tell the difference, and that scared me.

The last thing I wanted was to move forward with Seth if I wasn't a thousand percent sure. Any risk of losing him altogether, and it wasn't worth it. My phone buzzed again.

I guess I can swing past and grab some Chinese. But only doing this for Kahleesi.

I snorted and replied: *As if you'd have any chance with her.*

I set the phone down on the sofa. I needed to get

changed.

Twenty minutes later, he knocked on the door. I ran my brush through my hair and then sprinted to the door, swinging it open. He stood there holding Chinese, a lopsided grin on his face. My heart began to pound as I took in his appearance. He looked sexy, in an 'I just got home from work, threw on some clothes and haven't shaved in a week' kind of way. I resisted the urge to reach up and run my fingers over his stubble.

"Come in," I said, blushing. Was I turned on? Oh God, I'd forgotten what that felt like. It had been a *long* time since those kinds of feelings had been stirred inside of me.

"You get some drinks and I'll unpack this," he suggested.

I nodded, relieved that meant I could at least try and gather my composure in the kitchen.

"I got you honey chicken and chow mein because I wasn't sure what you were in the mood for."

I know exactly what I'm in the mood for.

Emily, stop it. I was mortified at myself. I shoved a soda into his hands and sat down in one of the armchairs, mainly so I didn't have to sit next to him. He raised an eyebrow at me.

"What?" I said, my defenses kicking in. I reached for the chicken and proceeded to shovel it into my mouth.

"Nothing," he chuckled. "Just in all the time you've lived here, I've never seen you sit anywhere but on the sofa."

I shrugged, like it didn't matter, but I couldn't help wondering what he meant by that. What was he thinking? Did he know I was sitting there because I didn't trust myself to sit close to him? My face burned.

"You're acting really weird, Em," he observed. "Care to share with the class?"

"No," I shot back. "And I'm not acting weird. I'm just tired. Long hours trying to catch up on the work I missed." I was getting desperate now, trying to steer the conversation into an area that felt safe.

"What's happening?" he asked, opening his beef. I sighed. It had worked. I babbled on about my column, and how they had changed ownership. My job was safe, but the freedom I'd had where I could basically work from wherever had gone. I now had a nine-to-five office job.

"Is that such a bad thing?" he asked, shrugging. "I mean, it gets you out of the house and mixing with people. After everything you've been through, maybe this is just what you need?"

"I guess you're right," I agreed. I hadn't thought about it like that.

Maybe he was right.

After dinner, I cleared away the trash and sat down on the sofa.

"Oh, so you're sitting next to me now?" he smirked. "I was beginning to think maybe I smelled or something."

"Well, I wasn't going to say anything..." I laughed as he swatted me.

My heart began to pound as I tried to psych myself up for what I was about to do. This was a big step. Telling him I had feelings for him was huge—something there was no going back from.

"I have something I need to say," I began. My voice trembled as it came out. Fuck, I was a mess.

"Are you okay?" His brow creased in concern.

Just say it. Tell him how you feel.

"I think I'm falling in love with you," I blurted out.

His eyes widened as he stared at me in shock.

Chapter Thirty-Three

Emily

"What?" The look on his face was priceless.

"I thought you wanted this. Maybe I was wrong. Forget I said anything…" I turned away, trying to hide my smile.

His fingers closed over my wrist as he swung me back so I was facing him. "No, Em. You don't get to tell me you're falling for me and then tell me to forget it." His voice was thick with emotion.

I gazed into his blue eyes and smiled. Why did this feel so awkward? I hadn't done the confessions of feelings since I was seventeen. You'd think it would get easier as you aged. It didn't. If anything, I felt more scared, more anxious than ever.

"Will you say something?" I said, unable to handle the silence any longer. The fact that I was pretty sure he felt the same did nothing to ease the mass of nerves in my stomach.

My fingers laced through his as I curved them around my back. The feel of his touch against my skin was incredible. It had been so long since I'd been intimate with anyone. Andy was the only guy I'd ever . . .

Thinking about him made me sad.

Nearly three months had passed since Andy's death. Seth had been wonderful. He had given me space when I needed it, and support when I was falling apart—which was still often.

I'd thought losing Andy would end my world. But life went on, whether I wanted it to or not. The world didn't stop just because I couldn't get out of bed.

"Just because a person has gone, it doesn't mean they won't live on in your heart forever."

Andy had told me that. After my parents had died, when I thought things would never get better, he'd made me realize that I had to go on. It was funny that it was his own words that were helping me now, nine years later.

"Are you sure you want this?" Seth whispered, tilting my chin until our lips met.

I nodded. Right then, I wanted it—*him*—more than anything. I needed him close to me.

He kissed me, his lips melting into mine as his fingers moved slowly through my hair. It was just a kiss, but it was so much more: it was a step forward. A sign, from me to Seth, that I could do this. That I *would* do it. For him.

"You have no idea how long I've wanted to do that," Seth muttered, pressing his forehead against mine. He kissed me again as though he thought at any minute I might realize my mistake and his chance would be gone.

"I . . . I can't promise that I can do this, but I want to try."

"If you're not ready, I'll wait, Em. I'll wait forever if I need to."

"No," I said, lifting my hand to his face, my fingers tracing along the length of his jaw. "I want this, Seth. And Andy would want it too." I wrapped my arms around his neck and pressed my lips against his. "And I mean that in the least creepy way possible," I added, making a face.

Seth laughed. "Sure you do, creepy girl."

I swatted his arm playfully. He sat down on the sofa, patting the seat next to him. I sat down and snuggled into his embrace.

That night, we did nothing more than kiss—though we did a lot of that. I wasn't going to rush it. Things would progress when we were both ready.

Chapter Thirty-Four

Seth

The door opened and Em stood there, smiling at me. She stepped forward and kissed me. "Don't you have a key or something?" she teased, raising an eyebrow.

I weaved my arm around her back and pushed her up against me. "No, I just know where you keep your spare. There's a difference."

"And the fact that you know that tells me what a true gentleman you are." She laughed. "Come on in. How do you feel about sushi?"

"I don't," I replied, screwing up my nose.

She laughed again. "Okay, pizza it is, then."

I shoved my hands in my pockets and watched her as she picked up the phone and ordered dinner. She looked fucking gorgeous in her gray silk blouse and charcoal skirt. She hung up the phone and I walked over to her.

"I would've eaten sushi for you," I commented with a grin.

Her lips lifted into a smile as her long, dark lashes closed and then opened, revealing those beautiful green eyes. "I know. But it's no fun if you're just going to sit there and screw up your nose." She dropped my hand and stepped toward the kitchen. "Do you want a drink?" she asked.

I nodded. "A beer would be nice."

She opened the bottle and handed it to me.

While we waited for dinner, we watched TV—or rather, she watched TV and I watched her, because even after a week of being together it still felt so unreal, as if any moment I was going to wake up and realize that this had all been in my head.

I ran my fingers over my pocket, trying to feel for the tiny charm I was hiding there. Still there. It was safe. I had no idea when the right time to give it to her was . . . or if there ever would be a right time. The last thing I wanted to do was make her sad. This had all seemed like such a great idea a couple of days ago.

The intercom buzzed. Em jumped up to answer it while I grabbed some plates from the kitchen. She came back into the living room carrying the pizza.

"We could've just used our hands." She laughed, her cheeks glowing with color as she rolled her eyes at the plates in my hands.

"And end up with crumbs everywhere? No way. You know how I feel about mess."

"Your mom hired you guys a maid in college because you were such slobs," she exclaimed, her mouth dropping open.

"Hey, that was all Andy, not me," I replied. "I was an innocent victim, forced to live in a health-hazard situation. Mom took pity on me."

Em laughed and shook her head. Taking two slices out of the box, she set them on her plate and handed the box to me. Our eyes met as my fingers brushed past hers. Even a simple touch from her sent my body into a spin. It was crazy, but from the way she'd jumped, and the color spreading across her face, I knew she'd felt it too.

We ate in silence. How was I going to do this? What if she reacted badly? I spied the bracelet as it hung over her left wrist, the delicate little charms rolling loosely around the fine silver chain. *Now. Just give it to her and get it over with.*

Just as I opened my mouth, she stood up and gathered our empty plates.

"Hey, come back here for a second." I grabbed her hand and pulled her down onto the armchair with me. She laughed as she fell into my lap. "Sorry," I muttered. Was this even a good idea?

"What are you doing?" She giggled, linking her hands around my neck. Her eyes met mine as she leaned in and kissed me. *God, her lips are so soft and sweet. I could go on kissing her forever.* Pressing my mouth against hers, I found myself wondering how in the hell I'd gotten so lucky.

Because Andy had died. If he were still around, then none of this would be happening. I pushed the thought from my mind. I couldn't think like that. If I let myself get inside my own head in that way, I'd ruin this. I'd ruin *her.*

"I wanted to give you something." Reaching into my pocket, I retrieved the black velvet pouch.

"What's this?" she asked, taking it from me. The color drained from her face. "I . . . it's not . . ."

My eyes widened as I realized what she was thinking. "God, no," I replied. I hadn't even thought that . . . She raised her eyebrows at my tone. "I mean, not that I don't want to marry you, but . . . just open the damn present." She had me flustered. I couldn't even get my words straight.

She laughed as she eased the tie loose and slipped her fingers inside. Her brow creased as she tipped the contents of the bag into the palm of her hand. A tiny little pink and silver ball fell out.

"Oh Seth, it's beautiful," she whispered. She held the charm in her hand, taking in all the tiny detail.

"It's called a memory charm," I began, "The top actually unscrews, and there is a tiny little hollow area inside. I went to Deb . . ." I cleared my throat. "There is a little piece of Andy in there. I wanted him to always be close to you. This way, he's always there."

She looked up at me, her eyes glistening with tears.

Throwing her arms around my neck, she hugged me, her arms gripping me tightly.

"That is the sweetest thing anyone has ever done for me."

"Even though we're trying this 'us' thing out, I never want you to feel like I'm trying to replace him," I said, holding her tightly.

"And I love you for that."

"I love you too, Em. You know that I'll always be there for you, right? No matter what happens with us, you'll always have me as a friend."

***

I stood in front of her as she sat on the end of the bed, my fingers raking through her silky hair. She gazed up at me, her eyes full of love. God, she was beautiful. Her hands moved around the back of my waist, dipping under my shirt. The feel of her nails moving over my skin was incredible.

"We don't have to do this," I said, touching her cheek.

"I want to." She stood up, her hands moving higher underneath my shirt.

Leaning down, I kissed her, my lips crushing against

hers. Lifting my shirt over my head, I let it fall to the ground. She smiled, letting her hands roam over my naked chest.

I kissed her as my fingers fumbled to unbutton her shirt. My hand ran down the center of her chest, over the top of her white, lacy bra. My heart beat loudly in my chest. Was this really happening? Pushing the shirt down over her shoulders, I kissed her neck, my tongue running over her sweet, soft skin. She gasped, shrugging the shirt free of her arms.

Reaching behind her, I unclasped her bra, moving the straps down her shoulders, over her creamy white skin.

"You're beautiful," I whispered, taking in her beauty. She smiled, lowering her eyes as my gaze ran over her full breasts. Reaching up, my finger circled around her nipple as it stiffened against my touch.

Lowering her onto the bed, I kissed her neck, then along her jaw, slowly making my way around to her mouth, my hardness brushing past her thigh. Reaching behind her, I unzipped her skirt and lowered it down over her hips.

She's so beautiful. I gazed at her below me, cupping her chin as my lips connected with hers. She reached down and unzipped my pants, freeing my erection. I groaned as her fingers closed around it, barely able to contain myself.

I shrugged off my jeans and boxer shorts and reached inside the drawer next to me for a condom. We kissed again, my lips wandering down her neck and over her breasts, curling my tongue around her left nipple.

"Oh," she gasped, arching her back. Moving her legs apart, I pushed myself between them, my erection resting against her wet entrance. Wrapping her arms around my neck, she locked her legs around my waist as I eased myself inside her.

"You okay?" I whispered, kissing her nose. She nodded as I pressed my forehead against hers as I gently rocked inside of her. As cliché as it sounded, she was perfect. Everything about her amazed me. Being with Em had felt like heaven, a place I never wanted to leave.

"How are you?" I asked her. She lay in my arms, smiling as my fingers stroked her arm, her naked body molded against mine like we were a perfect fit.

"I'm good," she said. "Better than good, actually. I'm great."

"You're better than great," I teased, tilting her head back

so I could kiss her.

She rolled her eyes, her lips lifting into a grin. "You're such a dork." She laughed, shaking her head. "But a loveable one."

I kissed her roughly, my mouth pressing against hers.

I could lie here all day, with her in my arms.

Chapter Thirty-Five

Emily

"Em, sorry to barge in—"

I sat bolt upright in bed, untwining my naked body from Seth's, and found myself staring into the shocked face of Deb. Her eyes darted from me to Seth and back to me before she bolted out of the room.

"Shit," I gasped, my heart racing.

I felt sick. Of all the things for her to walk in on, it had to be me and Seth in bed together? *Fuck, this is bad.* I jumped out of bed and reached for my robe, throwing it over myself.

"Seth, get up. Deb's here. She just walked in on us."

Seth's eyes flew open. He stared at me in shock. "Here? She's here? What the hell is she doing here?" He threw the covers off and made a beeline for his clothes, which were still lying in a heap on the floor.

"I don't know. She just walked in. She must've knocked and I didn't hear her." I ran my hands through my tangled hair. *How do I handle this?* Tightening the tie around my waist, I dashed out to the living room.

Deb sat perched on the edge of the sofa, her red eyes filled with anger. Crap. How could I expect her to understand?

"Deb . . ." My voice caught in my throat. I had no idea what to say. This wasn't what it looked like? Because it sure as hell was what it looked like. It had taken me less than three months to move on from losing Andy. I wanted to be sick. I sat down, clutching my stomach.

"How could you?" She turned to me, tears filling her eyes. In all the time I had known her, I'd never seen her look so cold.

"Deb, I can explain," I began.

"Can you? What could you possibly tell me right now that would make this okay? After all we've done for you . .

He loved you, Emily. Did you even love him?"

"I get that you're upset right now, but you have no right to question how I felt about Andy," I shouted.

Deb glanced up as Seth entered the room, her mouth twisting into a scowl. "And you," she raged, standing up. "He was your best friend." With her hands laced behind the back of her neck, she squeezed her eyes shut before shaking her head. "I can't be here. I can't even look at you." Snatching up her bag, she stormed toward the door.

I have to talk to her.

"Let her go," Seth said, grabbing my arm. "She's angry, Em. Nothing you say right now is going to make this okay. Let her calm down and then give her a call."

"I've never known Deb to hate anyone," I whispered. "But the way she just looked at me . . ." I couldn't even meet Seth's eyes, I felt so guilty. "You have to go."

"What?" His brow creased. "Go where?"

"Home. I can't have you here right now. I need time to think."

"Em, it'll be okay. She's angry. When she calms down and we explain it to her . . ."

I snorted. I could tell by the way he wouldn't meet my

eyes that even *he* didn't believe that. He reached for my hand. Jerking away, I shook my head. I felt dizzy. There were too many things running through my mind.

Maybe it's the universe telling us we shouldn't be together?

"Seth, please," I begged him, wrapping my arms around my waist. "If you don't leave, I will. Just give me some space."

"You can't push me away every time things get hard, Em."

"What?" I shook my head in disbelief. This was the first time I'd ever felt like he didn't understand me. "This isn't *nothing*. I'm not worrying about some stupid little thing. Deb is my family." I couldn't live with her hating me.

"And what am I?" he asked, his voice soft. He walked over and kissed me on the forehead. "I'll go, Em. I'll give you space, but know that tomorrow I'll be back here because I refuse to let you feel guilty about us. This is what Andy wanted." His eyes met mine, shadowed in pain. "What do *you* want, Em?" he asked.

I watched as he walked out, my heart leaping into my throat.

Him. I want him.

Chapter Thirty-Six

Seth

Fuck! I punched the steering wheel, my fingers throbbing in pain. I'd been sitting in my car for the last fifteen minutes, parked outside her apartment. *I shouldn't have left.* She would be tearing herself apart, feeling horrible for something that she shouldn't be feeling guilty about.

In the back of my mind, I had been stressing about people finding out. How could anyone really understand any of this? Was I really that surprised Deb had lost it? Of course not. Her son had died, and in her eyes we had moved on—only things were never that simple. We hadn't moved on; it was a new path we were taking together.

Andy had been a huge part of both our lives, and we would never forget him. The idea of people thinking that we loved him any less made me furious. What right did Deb—what right did *anyone*—have to judge our relationship?

***

This is a bad idea. I rapped on the door before I could change my mind. In my hands, I held the videos Andy had made during our trip. We hadn't had a chance to watch through them, but maybe if Deb could see us all together she would understand. Then again, maybe I was fooling myself.

The door opened and Deb stood there, frowning at me.

"This is not a good time, Seth."

"It's never going to be a good time." I crossed my arms over my chest to let her know I wasn't going anywhere until I'd said my piece. "She's sitting at home, blaming herself. This is the girl who dedicated her life to looking after and loving your son, and you go off at her like that?" I shook my head. "I get that you're upset, but you can't even begin to understand what she's going through."

"It's been weeks, Seth. *Weeks*. And then I walk in on

that? How did you expect me to react? I wanted you to look after her, not move in on her," she said, her lip curling in disgust. "What about Andy?"

"He wanted this," I growled, my anger growing. "She needs your support, Deb. She has nobody."

"She obviously has you," she shot back.

I shook my head. There was nothing I could say just then that was going to make it okay. I handed her the tapes.

"What are these?" she asked.

"The last few weeks of your son's life. Watch them and tell me she didn't love him enough." I walked off, not looking back. I refused to feel guilty about loving her. The only person I had to answer to was Andy, and I'd already done that. Deb could hate me all she wanted, but I needed her to forgive Em; because otherwise the guilt was going to end up killing her.

Chapter Thirty-Seven

Emily

I couldn't even imagine how awful that must have been for her. Walking in on Seth and I so soon after Andy had gone . . . in what world was that okay?

Her reaction had been a wake-up call. Nobody was going to understand us being together, least of all our families. If we were serious about being a couple, then that was something we needed to give them the opportunity to get used to.

So now I had a decision to make. Was the chance of finding love with Seth worth losing the people who had been my family for the past ten years? Because no matter how right it felt, or how much we knew we had Andy's blessing, they might never accept us being together.

"Em?"

I looked up from my bed and saw Seth standing there.

"I used the spare key," he explained. He looked uncomfortable, with his hands shoved deep into his pockets. He hesitantly took a step toward the bed and sat down.

"I've had enough of people helping themselves to my spare key," I mumbled, trying to make a joke. "That's it. I'm moving it."

He smiled. "I've just come from Deb's."

"And?" Not that I needed to ask. His lack of eye contact told me everything I needed to know. "She hates us, doesn't she? Not that I blame her."

"I refuse to let you feel guilty about us," he said, his voice gruff. He took hold of my hand and I sighed.

"That's just it. I feel bad for her seeing us like that, but guilt? No. I don't feel bad about us." I paused, wetting my lips.

"But?" he pushed, sensing my hesitation.

"But I don't know if that's enough." I sat up, pushing

my legs over the edge of the bed. "I've lost so many people close to me. How many more can I lose? I love you, I really do, but I don't know what to do here."

"Do what feels right," he said. "Does being with me feel right? If everyone was okay with us being together, then what would you want?"

"You," I whispered.

He moved closer until his mouth was on mine. But things weren't that easy, were they? I inhaled sharply when his fingers touched my neck. His lips synced against mine, then he moved slightly until our foreheads touched. I opened my eyes and stared straight into his.

"You know how I feel. I'll never leave you, Em."

I smiled. But as much as I loved hearing those words, I knew that sometimes life didn't give you a choice.

Chapter Thirty-Eight

Seth

"I've got something to say."

Opening my front door and seeing Em standing there, I'd been shocked.

"Come in," I said. I walked into the living room and sat down.

She followed, and perched herself in front of me on the edge of the coffee table. Her hands gripped the underside of the wooden frame. Her brow creased and she frowned, her expression serious.

We hadn't spoken much about Deb—or us—since the incident the week before. Nor had we heard from her. I was disappointed, but still hopeful that one day she would understand.

"You're worrying me," I said with a nervous chuckle. I reached out, my fingers brushing over her thigh before falling back into my lap.

"Don't worry," she assured me. My nerves settled, but I was still wondering why she was here. "I just wanted to do this right. I've been thinking a lot about us. I don't want to lose you, Seth. I don't think I could handle just being your friend, nor do I want to. I wish we had Deb's support more than anything, but I can't lose you too."

Relief washed through me. I was sure she had been about to end things with me. Hearing her say she wanted us to work made me happier than I'd been in forever.

"You don't know what it means to hear you say that," I muttered. Sitting forward, I took her face in my hands and kissed her.

Chapter Thirty-Nine

Emily

Six months later.

"What is it?" I asked Seth. He put his phone away and walked over to me.

"That was Deb. She wants to see us."

"Now?" My eyes widened. We hadn't communicated in more than six months, after she had made it clear we were no longer welcome in their life. What could she possibly have to say to us now?

"I said we would go." He looked as shocked as I felt. He pressed his hand against mine. "What could she want?" he asked, echoing my thoughts.

Nearly nine months had passed since I'd lost Andy. Not a day went by where I didn't think about him, but for the most part it was happy memories that occupied my thoughts. Having his support had made it easier to fall into a relationship with Seth.

Sometimes I thought about how different things would have been if he'd never gotten sick; if he were still here with us. How could I be so in love with Seth and still comprehend loving Andy if he were still around?

We pulled up out front of Andy's parents' house. It hadn't changed at all over the months. It felt so weird being back there, and not knowing what to expect made it even more nerve-wracking.

"Are you ready?" Seth asked, reaching for my hand.

I nodded. As ready as I was going to get, anyway. We got out and walked up the driveway up to the front door. With every step, a new wave of anxiety washed over me.

I held Seth's hand tightly as he rang the doorbell. The few seconds it took for Deb to open the door felt like years. She smiled, so I smiled back. Was I supposed to hug her?

Shake her hand? I stood there awkwardly, wishing I knew how to act.

She ushered us inside. "Thanks for coming."

"What's this about?" Seth piped up. He clutched my hand. He was worried about me, and I liked how protective he was being. We followed Deb into the living room and sat down.

She cleared her throat. "Firstly, I want to apologize. One, I shouldn't have invaded your space like that, and two, I didn't know the full story."

"Full story?" I repeated, confused.

She nodded. "It took me a long time to watch through the videos you left me," she said, looking at Seth. "But I did that today." She held up a disc. "Do you mind if I play this for you?" she asked.

I glanced at Seth, who shrugged.

We sat down on the sofa as Deb loaded the disc into the player. Why did I suddenly feel so sick? My heart ached as Andy's smiling face filled the screen.

"Mom. Firstly, I want to say I love you. Thanks to you and Dad for being amazing parents, not only to me, but to Em, too. You have no idea how much your love and support means to her. Which brings me to the whole point of this video." He glanced down, his lips pressed into a straight line. "See, I'm dying. I've fought hard, but this damn disease is going to beat me. But before it does, I'm going to do my damn best to make sure two of the people I love most in this world find each other."

I glanced at Seth, my mouth hanging open in shock. When had he done this? From how well he looked, it had to have been a few weeks before our trip. Seth shrugged, looking as confused as I was.

"I'm not sure if you're aware, but my best friend has been pining over this girl for the last fourteen years. I get it. I mean, she's pretty hot. But he never made a move because he cared too much about my happiness. And Em . . ." He laughed and shook his head, staring directly down the lens of the camera. "What can I say about Em? She's put me first for so long that this is the only way I can think of to repay her."

He glanced down, wetting his lips before continuing.

"So this is what I'm going to do: everything in my power to help them find each other. I want to die knowing that the girl I love is going to continue to be loved. I wish so bad that it was me who was getting to grow old with her, but it's not. Life sucks, and Em has suffered enough. I know it's going to be hard for you to understand, but please, Mom, please promise me you will try. You've lost me, please don't lose them too." He smiled at the screen. "I love you."

Deb stood up and ejected the disc. Her eyes were red and wet. So were mine.

"I've watched this about twenty times now," she admitted, wiping her eyes. "And every time I feel like I've let him down by shutting you out."

I stood up and walked over to her, wrapping my arms around her shoulders.

She began to sob. "I'm sorry, Em. I'm so sorry."

"Shh, it's okay." I glanced at Seth over her shoulder. He smiled at me, and right away I knew he was proud of me. "We understand, Deb. We really do. I'm just so glad to hear from you."

She pulled away from me and smiled, pushing her blonde hair from her eyes. "We have a lot of catching up to do, don't we?" she whispered.

"We do," I smiled.

**

Seth took my hand and pulled me into his arms. After spending the afternoon with Deb, we were back at my house—really *our* house, considering how much time he'd been spending there.

I giggled as his arms curled around my back, sneaking up under my skirt, his fingers brushing over my bare skin. I shivered, leaning up to kiss him.

"I love you, Em. I really fucking love you," he said, his voice husky. His lips found mine again in another deep kiss. "I feel like the luckiest man in the world."

"I love you too," I smiled, drinking in his kisses.

When I fell in love with Andy, I thought that life could not get any better. I'd been through so much with losing my parents, but somehow, we had found something so wonderful and so rare—an unconditional love for each other.

When I found out he was dying, my whole world crumbled. I couldn't imagine ever feeling happiness again. But somehow, through all that pain, Andy had brought Seth and I together.

Every second of every day I had Andy to thank for

helping me find Seth, because without his love and support—and his not-so-subtle little push—Seth and I just wouldn't be.

Epilogue

Dear Andy,

I miss you so much. Every day I wish I could pick up the phone and call you, just to hear your voice. I have so much to tell you, so I thought I'd write it down and hope that you can see it from up there.

So much has happened, I don't even know where to begin. After two years, Seth finally asked me to marry him. I said yes. The wedding will be in June; just a small event, basically just his family and yours. You know I've never enjoyed the spotlight.

You would have been proud of him and how he asked me—it was all very romantic. He went all out, arranging a big scavenger hunt that had me racing all over town looking for clues. I was sure I looked like an idiot—but I didn't care. At the final point, he was there, waiting down on one knee with your grandmother's engagement ring. He had wanted me to have a piece of you. He never lets me forget you.

We talk about you all the time as if you are still here—what Andy would think about this, or what you would say about that. Sometimes I can almost fool myself into imagining you're not really gone, and that any moment you'll walk through the door and take me in your arms. I miss your hugs, and your kisses, and the way you could always make me laugh. I miss you.

So that's what's happening with me. Seth made partner at the firm, and we just put a deposit on a new house. We need the extra room with the baby coming. Oh, that's right, I haven't mentioned that yet.

I'm 28 weeks along, with a little boy. We know he's a gift you've sent to us; a piece of you for us to love and watch grow. That's why we are going to name him Andrew. Every day, I will look at him and remember you.

I love you and miss you,

Forever yours,
Em xx

Acknowledgements

So many people for me to thank, I apologize in advance if I miss you. First and foremost, thank you to my family for their wonderful support. I wouldn't be where I am today without them.

Thank you to my readers. Every day I am humbled by all of you. The emails, the messages I receive blow me away. It's the best feeling in the world hearing someone enjoyed your book.

Thanks to the best editor Lauren, and my Amazing proofreader, Amy for all your hard work, and a big thanks to Ashley from Redbird Designs for yet another amazing cover. You guys rock!

Thanks to my wonderful street team for spreading the word about *Out of Reach*. You guys all rock! A big thanks to my beta readers, Kylie, Stephannie, Kristine, Kristin, and my mum. Your feedback helped make this book.

A huge special thanks to three of the best authors in the

world, Alison, Mia, and S Moose. Thanks to you guys for all your support and help. You guys are amazing.

***Always You, by Missy Johnson. Out now at all major
online retailers. See below for an excerpt.***

Synopsis:

I was thrilled when I was offered a graduate teaching
position at the prestigious Tennerson Girls Academy. At
twenty-three, this would be my first 'real' teaching
assignment. Working at the elite boarding school, home to
the daughters of some of the wealthiest people in the world,
was a great opportunity that I would've been stupid to pass
up.

One week into my new job, and I suddenly had no idea
why I chose high school…I was a seventeen-year-old boy
once, I knew how teenage girls behaved.

You can't even imagine the hell of trying to teach thirty
hormonal-driven seventeen-year-olds who have been
cooped up, away from any male contact.

I could handle the whispers every time I entered the room. I
could even handle the obvious attempts at gaining my
attention. What I couldn't handle was her…

Rich bitches and way too many rules. Was it any wonder
that I hated school?

Add to that the lack of male contact, and I was going
insane. Like literally. I wasn't used to this. A year ago I

was normal. I had a boyfriend, friends, and a loving family. There is nothing normal about me anymore, and nobody here lets me forget that.

My name is Wrenn, and I'm only here because my aunt took me in after what happened, but my aunt also happens to be the headmistress of this academy...Can you see my problem?

I'm hated for my lack of money, and I'm hated for who my aunt is.

Then he arrived. Dalton Reed. My new history teacher.

Slowly, he helped me see that even in the worst situations, there is always hope.

Excerpt:

He dropped me back at my car just before half ten. I was shocked at how late it was. We had been talking for hours. I felt so relaxed around him, yet at the same time, nobody had ever had me feeling so damn wound up.

"So, you still want to see this movie tomorrow?" he asked, raising an eyebrow.

"Are you asking me out?" I asked, my tone sweet.

"No. I'm merely trying to broaden the cinematic

knowledge of one of my students." His expression became serious. "Asking out one of my students would be incredibly unprofessional on my part, and unethical. I wouldn't take advantage of you like that."

"What if I wanted to be taken advantage of?" I moved toward him—very slowly, gauging his reaction. He held his breath as I edged closer, until our lips were almost touching. I paused, looking into his eyes, so desperately wanting to feel his lips against mine, but not wanting to step over that boundary without him wanting it equally.

He tilted his head so his lips brushed over mine, the sensation making me dizzy. His hand wandered up to my face, his fingers gently running along my hairline. Then suddenly my lips were crushed up against his with a passion even *I* wasn't expecting.

As quickly as it began, he was away from me, his eyes a mixture of lust, regret and confusion. I was a hot mess. My heart was beating out of control, I felt hot *and* cold and lightheaded. Thank God I was sitting down, or I was sure I'd have ended up fainting.

"I'm sorry, Wrenn. I shouldn't have done that," he said quietly.

"You didn't do anything I didn't want," I replied. He sat, his hands clenched tightly on the steering wheel, not speaking. "Will I see you tomorrow?" I asked.

He glanced at me, confused. "The movie," I reminded him.

He exhaled loudly. "Do you think that's a good idea?" he asked, raising his eyebrows.

"Maybe not, but I think we need to talk about this . . . " He nodded as my voice trailed off.

"I'll call you." His voice had softened, as had his expression. His eyes were no longer hard. I nodded, and got out of the car, closing the door. He drove off, and I stood there on the curb, staring until I could no longer see his taillights. Once he was gone, I stepped into my car.

I sat there, trying to digest what had just happened. Kissing him had evoked everything in me. I felt like a hurricane of feelings and emotions had ripped through my body, leaving me a muddled mess inside.

Loving Mr. Daniels, by Brittainy C. Cherry. Available at all major online retailors from May 13ᵗʰ, 2014

Synopsis:

To Whom it May Concern,

It was easy to call us forbidden and harder to call us soulmates. Yet I believed we were both. Forbidden soulmates.

When I arrived to Edgewood, Wisconsin I didn't plan to find him. I didn't plan to stumble into Joe's bar and have Daniel's music stir up my emotions. I had no clue that his voice would make my hurts forget their own sorrow. I had no idea that my happiness would remember its own bliss.

When I started senior year at my new school, I wasn't prepared to call him Mr. Daniels, but sometimes life happens at the wrong time for all the right reasons.

Our love story wasn't only about the physical connection.

It was about family. It was about loss. It was about being alive. It was silly. It was painful. It was mourning. It was laughter.

It was ours.

And for those reasons alone, I would never apologize for loving Mr. Daniels.

-Ashlyn Jennings

Excerpt:

Ashlyn.

I stood up and walked out of the office. In the hallway, I sighed when I saw Daniel standing outside his classroom. We locked eyes and I turned to go the other way. I heard his footsteps growing closer and I stood still.

"Can I help you?" I questioned inimically. In the history of bad first days of school, I had to hold the record for the worst one ever.

"Theo Robinson is in my first hour. I can already tell he

can be a real prick. And he's not the brightest kid." Daniel slid his thumb across the bridge of his nose. He glanced down the hallways to make sure no one was watching and moved an inch away from me—just to be safe. "He thought Macbeth was some kind of new McDonald's sandwich and scolded me for forcing him to study the manslaughter of cows." He snickered to himself, but he looked so sad.

"What are you doing?" I whispered.

He ran his hand over his face and cursed under his breath. Merged in an unutterable sadness and confusion, he shrugged. "I don't know." He frowned perplexedly. "I don't even know what this means."

"And you think I do? You think this is easy for me?"

"Of course not."

"Listen. It's not like anything really happened between us anyway," I lied. "I'll pretend it never happened," I lied again. "Only if you promise not to look past me as if I don't exist. I can deal with the bullies. I can't deal with you ignoring me."

His hand ran across his mouth before he crossed his arms and stepped a few inches closer to me. "Your eyes are puffy. I made you cry."

My skin prickled by his proximity. "Life made me cry."
I hugged my books closer to me and closed my eyes.
"*When we are born, we cry that we are to come to this
great stage of fools,*" I quoted from Shakespeare's King
Lear.

"You're the smartest person I've ever met."

I sighed. "You're the smartest person *I've* ever met." I
paused. "I'm not stupid, Daniel. I know that we…can't be
anything. And I would switch out of your class but Henry
made sure that I was placed in it."

"Yeah…" he said. "I just wish I didn't like you so
much."

I didn't know why, but I felt like crying when he said
that. Because I liked him too. We *had* connected on
Saturday. At least I had… He'd awakened me after I'd
been asleep for so long.

"I would never jeopardize your job," I promised. I didn't
know how it happened, but somehow we were closer, so
close that I could smell his clean soap from his shower that
morning. Did I step forward or did he? Either way, neither

of us was going to step back. I closed my eyes and allowed his scents to wash over me, bathing me in fantasy and false hope.

When my eyes reopened, I saw his stare, strong and determined. He took my arm and pulled me around a corner. We went through a door to an empty staircase. He glanced up and down the stairs before he pressed his mouth against mine. My lips instantly separated and my tongue twirled against his.

My fingers ran through his hair, bringing back my 'Joe's bar' Daniel and making Mr. Daniels disappear for a moment in time. His hand gripped around my back. Kissing him in the silent stairwell felt dangerous, but safe. Adventurous, however idiotic. Depressing, yet real.

When he withdrew his mouth from mine and stepped back, we both knew that what we had done couldn't happen again. He bit the corner of his mouth and shook his head. "I'm so sorry, Ashlyn." The bell rang before I could reply, and he went on his way and I went on mine.

Find Loving Mr. Daniels and other novels by Brittainy C. Cherry at:
Amazon.com | barnesandnoble.com | iTunes

Facebook at: www.facebook.com/brittainycherryauthor
Twitter at: www.twitter.com/brittainycherry

*Read below for an excerpt from the #1 New Adult
Romance VERY BAD THINGS by Ilsa Madden-Mills.*

Synopsis:

Born into a life of privilege and secrets, Nora Blakely has
everything any nineteen-year-old girl could desire. She's an
accomplished pianist, a Texas beauty queen, and on her
way to Princeton after high school. She's perfect. Or is she?

Leaving behind her million-dollar mansion and Jimmy
Choos, she becomes a girl hell-bent on pushing the limits
with alcohol, drugs, and meaningless sex.

Then through a chance encounter, she meets her soulmate.
But he doesn't want her.

When it comes to girls, twenty-five-year-old Leo Tate has
one rule: never fall in love. His gym and his brother are all
he cares about...until he meets Nora. He resists the pull of
their attraction, hung up on their six year age difference.

As they struggle to stay away from each other, secrets will
be revealed, tempers will flare, and hearts will be broken.

Welcome to Briarcrest Academy...where sometimes, the
best things in life are *Very Bad Things.*

Excerpt:

It took fifty-three seconds for him to appear beside me in the bar.

I sensed the anger pouring off him before he even sat down. "Not drinking today?" he said in a low voice.

"No fake ID," I said, putting my hand on his inner thigh and caressing the taut muscles there. "You seem tense. Is there anything I can do to help you relax?" I asked, my lips curving up.

He stared at my stroking hand and swallowed, but didn't move away. "I just came over to see how you're doing," he said with a stone-like face, not giving anything away.

I scowled and pulled my hand back. "Why? Because you feel bad for the poor little rich girl with all the problems?"

He looked away from me.

Yep.

I said, "Let's go in the bathroom and fuck."

He exhaled heavily and stood up from the stool.

"No?" I said, feeling all at once ashamed for the words coming out of my mouth, yet completely powerless to stop them. "You know, one of my favorite books has this sizzling, hot chapter where the main characters go to lunch together. And even though it's a first date, they end up in a bathroom stall, because they can't wait to get at each other. He just bends her over and gives it to her, hard and fast. I'd like to reenact that scene." I took a hasty sip of water and got my nerve up. "All we'd have to do is pick the biggest stall, and then you flip my dress up and take me from behind. Or I could get on my knees for you? I'd suck you, if you like."

He paled and pinched the bridge of his nose. "You don't want me, Nora. I'll fuck you, and when I'm done, I'll leave you."

At the thought of him leaving me, all the air was taken out of me and a pain squeezed my heart so hard I thought I might cry out. "Well if not you, then someone else will do," I said with a shrug, looking around the bar. "Who should I choose? There's the young guy over there in the corner with the power suit and buzz cut who's been trying to catch my eye since I sat down . . . although I think I see a wedding band on his hand. He's out, I suppose. Even I have standards. And, there's the fortyish-looking guy sitting across from me. He's been staring at my breasts." I smiled and waved at the gentleman in question, and he waved back, a hopeful look on his face. "Oh yeah, definitely interested."

I opened my purse and pulled out a pen and wrote my name and number on a bar napkin. I pushed it over to Leo. "Do me a favor? Take this over to him and tell him what a great girl I am. How good I am. How you know I'm not really bad." I stared at the bulge in his pants. "Maybe tell him how hard you get when I talk about fucking."

Very Bad Things is a complete standalone novel without a cliffhanger.

Amazon: http://amzn.to/1ed1rVN

Barnes & Noble: http://bit.ly/1bOyH2g

Ilsa's website: http://www.ilsamaddenmills.com/

FB: https://www.facebook.com/authorilsamaddenmills

MISSY JOHNSON

CPSIA information can be obtained
at www.ICGtesting.com
Printed in the USA
LVOW12s2207190717

541894LV00004B/821/P